AFTER THE STORM

Also by Maggie Dana

TIMBER RIDGE RIDERS
∾ Book Eight ∾

AFTER THE STORM

Maggie Dana

PAGEWORKS PRESS

After the Storm © 2013 Maggie Dana
www.timberridgeriders.com

ISBN 978-0-9851504-7-1

Edited by Judith Cardanha
Cover by Margaret Sunter
Interior design by Anne Honeywood
Published by Pageworks Press
Text set in Sabon

In memory of my father

1

SITTING CROSS-LEGGED on her rumpled bed, Holly Chapman leaned forward and jabbed her laptop's refresh button so hard that its screen almost jiggled.

"C'mon, c'mon," she said.

But nothing changed. The show's web page remained exactly as it had been all day—photos of horses and interviews with trainers . . . but no results. They'd been promised for two o'clock that afternoon. Yet here it was almost seven on Monday night, and Holly still didn't know for sure if her best friend, Kate McGregor, had made the final cut for the Festival of Horses.

She had to. She absolutely *had* to.

Kate's rival, Angela Dean, claimed to have inside information and she'd already announced that she and Kate had qualified, but Holly didn't trust her. Angela

1

wouldn't know the truth if it cantered up on a Grand Prix horse and kissed her.

Tucking a wedge of blond hair behind one ear, Holly tackled her laptop again. This time, an error message popped up. Maybe Kate was having better luck. She lived in the village where the Internet connection was stronger. Holly grabbed her cell phone and punched in Kate's number. It rang twice, then switched to voice mail.

That was odd.

Kate always carried her iPhone in case her boyfriend, Nathan, called. He was an actor and he'd been on location in New Zealand since early September filming *Moonlight*, a movie based on Holly's favorite fantasy book about horses with wings, and—

Duh-uh.

No wonder Kate hadn't answered. She was at her father's butterfly museum helping with a birthday party for middle school kids. Ben McGregor had banned cell phones from the conservatory in case their radio waves or gamma rays or whatever upset his rare butterflies and moths.

Holly's mom, Liz, stuck her head around Holly's bedroom door. "Any news?"

"Not yet."

"It'll be up soon," Liz said. "There's probably a glitch with the software."

"Or with Mrs. Dean," Holly muttered.

Angela's mother was famous for pulling strings when it came to Angela winning prizes. According to barn gossip, Mrs. Dean had once bribed a judge. Maybe she was emailing the show officials at that very moment, holding everything up while she made sure that Angela qualified for the Festival of Horses in April. Holly had already qualified in mid-December, and so had Jennifer West, another Timber Ridge rider. Last weekend's show was Kate's turn.

Liz frowned. "I'm still mad at you girls for sneaking off."

"We didn't," Holly said. "We told Aunt Bea, and she came with us. Kate's therapist said her knee would be fine."

"You should've told me," Liz said.

"And you'd have stopped us."

"Maybe."

"But Mom," Holly wailed, "it was Kate's last chance to qualify."

They'd been arguing about this since the previous night when Liz got home from her weekend in Boston. She hadn't wanted Kate to compete because of her bad knee. She had no idea that the girls had gone to the show until she called Holly on Saturday afternoon to check on things at the barn and discovered that Kate had just ridden a brilliant dressage test on Holly's horse, Magician.

Holly had taken a video of Kate's performance, so she fired it off quickly to her mom and then handed her phone to Aunt Bea. It had taken all of Aunt Bea's considerable powers of persuasion to stop Liz from having a major meltdown.

She looked ready to argue again when her cell phone rang and Mrs. Dean's voice blared into Holly's bedroom like an irritated foghorn. Mom must've hit the speaker button.

"Have you seen the results?" demanded Mrs. Dean. She ruled the Timber Ridge Homeowners' Association with an iron fist, and when she issued commands, everyone jumped—even Mom.

"We're looking now."

"Don't bother," Mrs. Dean said. "Angela has qualified. I *told* you she would."

"What about Kate?" Liz said, running a hand through her tousled blond hair. It stuck up behind her ears and reminded Holly of Plug's defiant little forelock that refused to lie down no matter how many times you brushed it. Plug had taught her to ride, and he was still teaching beginners at the barn.

"I didn't look," Mrs. Dean said and hung up.

* * *

With a sigh of relief, Kate McGregor helped parents round up the last few kids and herd them out the door. The children had already ransacked the museum's gift shop like a swarm of locusts, scooping up butterfly pins, bug boxes, and cocoon hatching kits. Kate's father had signed his latest book for birthday girl and given each child a sticker with the museum's name—"Dancing Wings."

Kate flopped onto a bench and wiped a strand of sweaty brown hair off her forehead. Dad kept the butterfly conservatory at tropical temperatures, and chasing after all those kids had been hot work. They'd happily ignored her father's rules about no running or shouting, and a couple of parents had needed reminders to turn off their cell phones.

Remembering hers, Kate pulled it out. Two messages—a reminder from Liz about tomorrow's riding lesson and a text from Holly. *Nothing yet*, it said above a row of yellow frowny faces.

Kate's left knee began to throb.

Four weeks ago she'd injured it while skiing with Brad Piretti, and everyone—including her doctor and Liz—said she wouldn't be able to compete in the horse show. Even Kate had had doubts.

But Holly believed she could do it.

So Kate had exercised like crazy—lifting weights, pounding the elliptical machine, and swimming laps every day after school. And when her dad had taken Liz away last weekend, Holly had hatched a scheme that would get Kate to the show without their parents knowing . . . at least not till it was all over and they couldn't do anything about it.

So far, the only fall-out was from Liz who'd threatened to banish Kate and Holly from the barn for a week. But after much pleading, she'd finally relented and told them they had to clean out her office instead.

Dad hadn't said a word, but then he rarely did unless whatever Kate had done compromised his precious butterflies.

Kate's cell phone buzzed.

Up came Holly's number, but Kate hesitated. Maybe it was bad news, like she'd totally flubbed it up and Angela had lied about her qualifying, or—

"You're in!" Holly squealed.

"Seriously?"

"Yes, seriously."

Ignoring her knee, Kate leaped to her feet and half ran, half limped into the gift shop. Pop-up books, video games, and stuffed caterpillars spilled from shelves; wooden puzzles ran amok over the counter. A butterfly mobile dangled above Dad's head as he tried to restore order with the help of Mrs. Gordon, his new assistant.

A halo of frizzy black hair framed Mrs. Gordon's pale face, and her teeth gleamed like tombstones in the shop's overhead lights. Kate gave a little shudder. No wonder kids called her "The Gorgon."

Dad coughed. "What's wrong?"

"Nothing," she yelled, waving her phone. "I qualified."

For a moment, he looked puzzled, as if he'd forgotten all about the show. But Kate was used to that. Dad was so wrapped up in his butterflies that the real world barely existed for him. He'd always been this way, even when Mom was alive.

"Oh, right—"

But The Gorgon cut him off. "That was very naughty of you, Kate, going to the show without permission," she said, sounding just like the high school principal she once was. "Your poor father was frantic with worry."

Hardly, Kate thought. *He was in Boston having fun with Liz.*

It's what she and Holly had been hoping and planning for. They wanted their parents to get married so they'd be a real family and Kate and Holly would be real sisters as well as best friends. But Mrs. Gordon had come to work at the museum and derailed their plans by making herself indispensable to Kate's father.

"Yes, well," he said, tugging at his beard—a sure sign he didn't know how to handle something.

Kate said, "Aren't you pleased?"

Silently, she urged her father to stand up for himself. He was a world-famous lepidopterist, and he'd led scientific expeditions to the Amazon jungle, survived three bouts of malaria, and confronted spiders the size of knapsacks, but he crumpled like a first-grader beneath Mrs. Gordon's critical stare.

Briskly, she said, "Ben, what should we do with these butterfly puzzles? The kids have ruined them."

* * *

At lunch time on Tuesday, the riding team celebrated Kate's success in the school cafeteria.

"Cool beans," said Jennifer West, tucking into a bowl of chili. Her spiky red hair was all set for Valentine's Day. On St. Patrick's Day, Holly predicted, Jennifer's hair would be greener than a shamrock.

Sue Piretti grinned. "I knew you'd make it."

"So did I," said Robin Shapiro.

To help Kate get to Larchwood, Sue and Robin had both volunteered to stay behind at the barn, mucking out stalls and feeding horses while Brad had borrowed a neighbor's horse trailer and driven Kate to the show. Holly's boyfriend, Adam Randolph, had reserved a stall for Magician at the Larchwood barn, Jennifer had handled all the paperwork, and Holly had propped Kate up with promises that Magician would carry her to victory.

This was just a qualifying show. Riders either passed or failed, and there were no ribbons, so Aunt Bea had knitted one that she pinned to Magician's bridle. He was Holly's horse, but Kate loved him as much as she loved her own horse, Tapestry.

"Thanks again," Kate said, feeling herself blush. "I couldn't have done it without you guys."

"Including me?" said Brad Piretti.

Balancing two trays, the high school's star quarterback squeezed himself into a chair between Kate and Robin. His long legs barely fit beneath the table.

"You hungry, bro?" Sue asked, eyeing his mountain of food—two mammoth burritos, a double serving of fries, and an extra-large soda.

He shrugged. "A guy's gotta eat."

Kate was about to thank Brad too, when giggles

erupted from a table across the aisle. Kate turned and found Angela Dean's icy blue eyes boring into her like a dentist's drill. A mocking smile lifted the corners of Angela's pouty mouth.

She sat with her cousin Courtney and her best friend, Kristina James. They wore matching outfits—green tops that barely covered their midriffs and short green skirts with yellow stripes.

"The Pom Pom Squad," Holly muttered.

Jennifer snorted. "Cheerleader Barbies."

"Hey, wait a minute," Brad protested. "They're—"

Sue glared at him. "What?"

"The guys play better when—"

"Pfftt," Sue said. "Riders don't need cheerleaders. Only dumb football players do."

"Okay, fine," Brad said, shrugging. "But we think they're pretty awesome."

In a flash, Sue leaned across the table and punched her brother so hard that he fell off his chair. Root beer flew in one direction, french fries in the other, and Brad landed on the floor looking kind of surprised to find himself there.

Kate bit back a smile.

Poor Brad. He didn't deserve this. He really had been hugely helpful. If he hadn't volunteered to drive the trailer, she'd never have gotten to the show. Despite Sue's angry stare, Kate reached down to help him up.

* * *

Snowflakes the size of cotton balls swirled past Kate's window as she rode the school bus with Holly. Ahead, two plows cleared a path in the narrow road, already down to one lane of traffic.

Was this a mistake?

Maybe she should've blown off Liz's lesson and gone home instead. But Kate was anxious to get back in the saddle. Tapestry hadn't been ridden in six weeks, thanks to Kate's bum knee. And thanks to the bad weather, she'd been cooped up inside a stall as well. Ever since Halloween there'd been one snowstorm after another, and the horses couldn't be turned outside because the paddocks were like skating rinks, buried beneath layers of ice.

The bus lurched around a corner.

Leaning into the aisle, Kate peered through the front windshield. Timber Ridge Mountain towered above them. With its frosted pine trees and red barns, the mountain was a travel poster for Vermont—right down to the snow-covered trails that spilled from its peak like dribbles of white paint. One of them was

11

called "Nightmare," the black diamond run where Kate had gotten hurt.

It was only her second time on skis, and even though she was nervous about falling, she wanted to try again. Maybe on Valentine's weekend. It was less than two weeks away and all the girls were buzzing with excitement about the school dance and obsessing over whether they'd get cards from guys they liked.

Kate had never gotten a Valentine, not from a boy, anyway, and she didn't expect any this year. Nathan would be on his way back from New Zealand and probably wouldn't even realize what the date was. As for Brad Piretti, well, he wasn't a boyfriend, even though Holly never stopped teasing her about him.

Turning around, Jennifer grinned at Holly. "Adam knows you'll kill him if he doesn't send you a Valentine."

Sue nodded. "He'd be dead meat."

"Ugh," said Robin. "That's disgusting."

"You'll get two," Holly said, giving Kate a good nudge. "One from dreamy Nathan Crane and one from Brad who's not quite so dreamy, but—"

"Hey, that's my brother," Sue said. "He's—"

"—still mad at you for punching him," Robin retorted.

Someone from the back of the bus yelled out.

"What did the boy bird say to the girl bird on Valentine's Day?"

Jennifer turned. "Okay, shoot."

"Let me call you tweet heart."

Everyone groaned; then Robin held up her hand. "Okay, so why did the banana go out with the prune?"

"Because it couldn't get a date," Holly said.

Brakes squealing, the bus stopped.

There was a mad scramble for knapsacks as Jennifer and Robin jumped off and headed toward Timber Ridge Manor. Angela lived there as well, in a three-story mansion with massive stone lions that guarded its front door, but she never rode the bus. Her mother or a hired driver would always pick her up from school.

At the next stop, Holly and Kate got off. The Chapmans' modest house had weathered shingles, window frames in need of paint, and a ramp at the front door, left over from when Holly was in a wheelchair. Kate had lived there from June to Thanksgiving the previous year, but she'd never ceased to marvel at Holly's bedroom every time she walked through the door.

"Wow," she said, the way she always did.

Holly grinned. "Over the top, huh?"

"Kind of," Kate said, grinning back.

Not an inch of wall space showed beneath posters of show jumpers, eventers, and dressage horses. Magician, in a collage of photos, filled Holly's corkboard; ribbons—mostly blue—framed her mirror. Others hung like bunting around both windows.

On the bookshelf, sandwiched between stacks of *Practical Horseman* and Pony Club manuals, a Breyer colt stuck his handsome head out of a model barn. Stuffed ponies snoozed amid a nest of bed pillows. Wild horses galloped across the ceiling.

Holly plucked her chaps off a wooden rocking horse and straddled it. "So, what are you going to do about the Valentine dance?" she said.

Kate blinked. "Huh?"

"Don't play dumb," Holly said. "Brad's going to ask you."

"How do you know?"

"Sue told me."

2

KATE CAUGHT HER BREATH. This was a conversation she didn't want to have, not even with Holly. She liked Brad. He was well over six feet tall and had curly brown hair, mossy green eyes, and shoulders so wide it looked as if he were wearing football pads, even when he wasn't.

Brad was also learning to ride, and Kate really liked that. But she already had a boyfriend—well, sort of—and everyone at school thought it was super cool because Nathan Crane was a movie star. But they didn't understand the dynamics.

Nathan spent most of his life in the world of make-believe, thousands of miles away. He'd once been an ordinary teenager, living in Vermont and goofing around in school plays with Holly's boyfriend, Adam—until a talent scout lured him away. After that, Nathan's acting career took off . . . like into the stratosphere.

His latest text was from Hawaii where he and his co-star, the impossibly glamorous Tess O'Donnell, were enjoying a quiet vacation before heading back to Hollywood. The gossip mags were all over it.

Romantic Getaway, screamed one headline.

Another said, *What's Up with These Two?*

Holly insisted it was just a publicity stunt. "It's what Nathan's fans want," she'd said. "It means nothing, so ignore it, okay?"

Kate did her best. But right now, Holly's vivid blue eyes weren't letting her ignore the fact that Brad Piretti was about to ask her out . . . *again.*

Somehow, Kate had neatly sidestepped Brad's previous invitations without hurting his feelings, but she didn't have a clue how to sidestep this one. Was it okay to pretend that she was allergic to red satin hearts or couldn't cope with loud music?

Probably not.

Okay, so some people were scared of clowns. Kate wasn't, but she could easily fake it. Maybe she could make a big deal about being scared witless by masks.

That's what all the kids were wearing.

The party's theme was *Secret Valentine*. The longer you kept your identity a secret, the better. Prizes would be awarded for the most original masks. The guys had groaned and thought it was stupid, but the girls loved it. Holly had already primed her glue gun and assembled an impressive collection of feathers, sequins, and beads.

"So, will you go?" she said.

"To the party?"

"Where else?" Holly said, rolling her eyes. "And quit stalling."

"I'm not," Kate said.

But she was. Parties with boys made her nervous, even though she'd been to more of them in the past six months than she ever had before. Oddly enough, they'd all been costume parties, including last week's Hawaiian luau at the Timber Ridge clubhouse and Holly's fifteenth birthday party in November.

That was Adam's idea.

He'd come up with the theme—a *Holly*wood party for Holly because she loved glamour and old movies. The guys rented tuxedos and the girls wore old-fashioned ball gowns they'd found at the thrift shop. The whole thing was a smashing success until Angela crashed the party with her cousin and set off all the fire alarms, like on purpose.

Except nobody could prove it was Angela.

With an exasperated sigh, Holly tossed Kate's barn

clothes at her. "C'mon," she said, pulling on a pair of old breeches. "Mom's waiting."

* * *

Horses whickered and rattled feed buckets as both girls entered the barn. Kate patted Daisy's black-and-white nose, rubbed Marmalade's enormous ears, and then stopped at Plug's stall. Always on the lookout for food, the little brown pony nuzzled her hand.

"Forget it," she scolded. "You're too fat."

Plug gave a loud sigh as if he understood. He reminded Kate of a Thelwell pony—round and fuzzy and incredibly smart. He could open his door faster than a cat burglar, which is why Liz kept it double bolted. The last time Plug got out, they caught him in the feed room, about to jailbreak the grain bins.

After planting a kiss on Plug's cute little nose, Kate slipped into Tapestry's stall. She wrapped her arms around the mare's warm neck and forgot all about Brad Piretti, errant boyfriends, and the school's Valentine dance. As she breathed in Tapestry's wonderful horsey smell, the rest of her bothersome world drained away like sand through an hourglass.

In the next stall, Holly fed carrots to Magician, her magnificent black gelding. He whuffled them up like a vacuum cleaner, then pushed his velvety nose into Holly's pockets, hoping for more.

Someone giggled. "Hey, stop that."

Kate turned and caught sight of Tara, Sue's Appaloosa mare, standing on the crossties and nibbling at Sue's sandy-colored hair.

"Tara thinks it's a carrot," Robin said.

Sue snorted. "It's not *that* red."

"No, it's orange," Robin said and ducked behind Chantilly's dappled gray rump before Sue had a chance to throw something at her.

Robin and Sue were best friends, the way Kate and Holly were best friends—Angela and Kristina, too, Kate supposed. The only girl at the barn without a best friend was Jennifer, but she didn't seem to need one. Everyone liked her . . . well, except for Angela who didn't like anyone. Kate wasn't sure Angela even liked Kristina James, despite claiming they were the best friends *ever*.

Liz yelled at everyone to hustle. "Lesson in ten minutes."

Pulling off Tapestry's blanket, Kate got busy with brushes, curry comb, and hoof pick. Tapestry's flaxen mane and tail shone like spun gold. Her heavy winter coat was the color of a newly minted penny. She stood at fifteen-three—an inch below Magician, but taller than most other purebred Morgans.

Kate was tacking up when Angela sauntered down the aisle. Wearing spotless buff breeches and custom-made boots, she complained loudly that nobody had bothered to groom Ragtime.

"That's *your* job," Liz said.

Kate and Holly traded looks.

This was typical behavior. Angela never groomed or tacked up her own horse if she could get someone else to do it for her. She stood outside Ragtime's stall, tapping her well-shod foot. Moments later Kristina James abandoned Cody, her palomino gelding, and ran up with Angela's grooming box and Ragtime's saddle. Angela gave Kristina a fake smile.

"Nice," Holly muttered.

Kate pulled a face. "Not."

Looking hopeful, Ragtime whickered and stuck his handsome bay head into the aisle. He'd frisk anyone for a treat, but Angela ignored him the way she'd ignored Skywalker, her previous horse. To her, they were nothing more than tickets to the trophies and blue ribbons that Mrs. Dean demanded for the money she spent on Angela and her horses.

It was the same with tennis and skiing.

If Angela didn't win, and win big, her mother complained to anyone who'd listen. And who knew what Angela endured behind closed doors? She'd arrive at the barn, tight-lipped, and pretend it didn't matter.

Kate felt a pang of sympathy.

Mothers were supposed to support their kids, not throw them under the bus. Her own had been right behind her until the day she died.

A tiny tear trickled down Kate's cheek. Wiping it away, she bottled up Mom's memory and finished grooming Tapestry.

* * *

With an exuberant squeal, Tapestry dropped her nose and bucked her way across the indoor arena. Kate barely managed to stay on. She was about to shove herself back in the saddle, when Tapestry bucked again. Taken by surprise, Kate went sailing over the mare's head. She landed with a whump, curled herself into a ball, and rolled sideways to protect her head.

In seconds, Liz was beside her. "You okay?"

"Yeah," Kate gasped. "I think so."

"Don't move," Liz said. "Catch your breath first."

Kate sucked in a lungful of air, then another. It felt like she'd been trapped under water. Finally, the arena walls stopped spinning. Had she banged her head? Probably not. The ground was soft, and her helmet was still securely in place.

With Liz's help, Kate managed to sit up. Her knee gave a small twinge, but nothing else hurt—except for her pride. From the corner of her eye, she saw Holly jumping off Magician and reaching for Tapestry's loose reins.

Moments later, something nudged her.

"Tapestry wants to apologize," Holly said, as the mare rested her whiskery nose on Kate's shoulder. "She's really, really sorry and promises never to do it again."

"Dream on," Liz said.

She stood up and hauled Kate to her feet, and Kate knew exactly what was coming next.

Get back on your horse.

People had been saying this ever since the first human climbed onto a horse's back, only to get promptly tossed off. Even Alexander the Great had been dumped by Bucephalus more than once, and Kate was willing to bet that someone had said these words to Alexander as well.

Brushing tanbark off her breeches, Kate flexed her left knee. Another twinge, but nothing she couldn't live with. Liz gave her a leg-up. Ears pricked, Tapestry snorted and skittered sideways.

"She's frisky," Liz said.

Kate shoved both feet in her stirrups and gathered up her reins. "No kidding," she said as Tapestry let off another playful buck.

"Ride 'em cowboy," Sue yelled.

Jennifer trotted past on Rebel, her flashy chestnut gelding. "Aunt Judith would love this," she said.

Kate managed a wry smile.

They'd all heard the stories about Jennifer's indomitable great aunt. She'd abandoned her English upbringing at the age of eighteen and run off to America to join a rodeo. For nine months Judith had toured with a flea-bitten outfit all over the mid-West, riding broncs, performing flips and backbends like Calamity Jane, and standing upright on two horses at a steady gallop.

Aunt Judith was a pistol.

Her twin sister, Caroline West, had once ridden for the British team and now owned Beaumont Park, one of England's most prestigious equestrian centers. She'd invited Holly and Kate to fly over that summer with Jennifer to attend a special program for talented young riders. With luck, Great Aunt Judith would be there, too.

* * *

The afternoon's lesson went from bad to worse, and no matter how hard Kate tried, she couldn't find her rhythm. Tapestry picked up the wrong lead, balked at the brush jump, and almost blew a gasket over a couple of orange traffic cones she'd seen a hundred times before. Kate even wound up posting on the wrong diagonal.

"Take a break," Liz said, sounding frustrated.

Angela smirked. "Ooooh, bad luck."

Riding past Kate, she pushed Ragtime into a flawless extended trot, and he floated across the arena like a fourth-level dressage horse, which he probably was. Nobody knew what Mrs. Dean paid for him, but it had to be a lot. Warmbloods like Ragtime didn't come cheap.

"Duh-uh," Holly said, when she joined Kate. "Of course Tapestry's a spaz. Nobody's ridden her since when . . . like Christmas?"

Gloomily, Kate nodded. "Yeah."

It had been a crazy six weeks. First, Kate had been banned by Mrs. Dean from riding in the December show. Then Magician had pulled up lame at the last minute, so Holly had ridden Tapestry instead. And a few days later, when the Festival Committee announced there'd be another show in late January, Holly had promptly offered Magician to Kate.

So they'd swapped horses.

Okay, that was cool—until Kate injured herself skiing right before New Year's and couldn't ride at all.

But Holly refused to give up. She'd stopped riding Tapestry and devoted all her spare time to schooling Magician so Kate would have the best possible chance of success. If Kate could get herself fit enough to compete in the January show, Holly promised that Magician wouldn't let her down. And he didn't.

Kate winced as her knee twinged again.

"You okay?" Holly said, kicking her feet free of the stirrups.

"I guess."

"You want to ride Magician?"

"Like right now?" Kate said.

"Yes."

"Sure, but why?"

"Duh-uh," Holly said again. "Because you'll be riding him at the Festival, remember? Not Tapestry."

That's what the rules said.

You had to ride the horse you qualified on, which was fine because Kate loved riding Magician. But it wasn't the same as riding her own horse. She knew Holly felt the same way. This show was a big deal—a very big deal—and rumor had it that scouts from the United States Equestrian Federation would be there, on the lookout for junior talent.

Kate was about to switch horses with Holly when Liz pointed to the far end of the arena. "Go and work off Tapestry's energy down there," she said. "Lots of big circles and keep her on the rail. She's not listening to you, so make her pay attention, okay?"

Feeling miserable, Kate nodded.

It was like getting a time out.

* * *

When the lesson was over, Liz called for a meeting in her office. "Thirty minutes," she said and strode off to deal with a hay delivery.

"What's all that about?" Kate said.

She'd finally gotten the kinks out of Tapestry, and the mare had settled down. She no longer shied at the traffic cones but still gave the chicken coop a wide berth.

Not surprising, really.

She'd once shared a weedy paddock with a flock of hungry hens that pecked at anything that moved. They belonged to a crazy old hermit who lived in a shack on the other side of Timber Ridge mountain. He'd stolen

Tapestry from the farm in New York where she'd been raised.

Tapestry's original name was Serenade and her legal owner, Richard North, was so grateful to Kate for rescuing his mare from the kill auction that he'd given Tapestry to her free and clear . . . but with one proviso. When Kate went off to college, she would allow Tapestry to be bred to Maestro, Mr. North's prize stallion, and he would get first refusal on the foal.

Holly had already dubbed it Arpeggio.

"This meeting's probably about the Festival," Holly said, walking beside Kate as they cooled off their horses.

Four Timber Ridge riders had qualified. This meant that Liz had an even bigger workload. Besides coaching them for the Festival, she still had to teach riding, run the barn, conduct clinics, and keep Mrs. Dean from driving everyone nuts.

Angela cantered by.

She'd flubbed up so badly at the December show that her mother had sold Skywalker, Angela's old horse, and bought Ragtime who was ten times better and probably cost ten times as much. Angela hadn't known about the deal until she got back from her winter ski vacation and found a brand-new horse in her stall.

But it did the trick.

Riding Ragtime, Angela had no trouble qualifying the second time she tried.

3

AFTER THEIR LESSON, the girls crammed themselves into Liz's small office. Robin and Sue shared a tack trunk, Jennifer snapped open a folding chair and sat on it backward, and Kate and Holly squeezed into Liz's old recliner that she'd rescued from the town dump.

Angela kept her distance.

Looking terminally bored, she leaned in the doorway, leg bent with one foot on the frame as if she were ready to bolt. Behind her, Kristina picked crimson polish off her nails.

"Will this take long?" Angela said.

"Why?" Holly said. "Got a hot date?"

"If you *must* know," Angela drawled, "Mother's taking me to Blaines for a fitting."

"Blaines?" Kate said. "What's that?"

Angela sniffed. "It's a boutique in Winfield. I'm getting a custom-made gown."

"What for?" Holly said.

"The Valentine Dance, stupid."

Holly burst out laughing. "It's a high school party," she said, "not a debutante ball."

"Well, *I'm* getting *my* dress from the thrift shop," Jennifer announced.

Robin said, "Me too."

"So am I," said Sue. She waved at Kate and Holly. "Let's all go, like we did last time. It'll be a blast."

"Peasants," Angela muttered. "You're—"

"Sorry I'm late," Liz said.

Gobs of snow fell from her jacket as she elbowed her way into the room and looked for a place to sit. Jennifer offered the metal chair, but Liz shook her head and perched on the edge of her desk. A box of paperclips clattered onto the floor, followed by broken pencils and a tube of worming paste. Immediately, Robin bent to pick them up.

"Thanks, but don't bother," Liz said. "Holly and Kate are going to clean up this weekend."

Robin gave a shy smile. "Okay."

"Now, I'm sure you've already heard," Liz went on, "but Angela and Kate have also qualified for the Festival, so congratulations." She smiled at both girls, even though Angela was studiously ignoring her. "And you all know what this means, right?"

Holly rolled her eyes. "Work, work, and—"

"—more work," Jennifer finished.

"It also means cooperation," Liz said. "That's been a bit thin on the ground lately, so I want you kids to pull together. This is a team effort, okay?"

"Wrong," Angela said. "It's individual."

"Then go by yourself," Holly snapped. "Let's see how you make out without a flunky to groom Ragtime, and—"

"That's enough, Holly," her mother said.

Angela tossed back a wave of coal black hair. "Are we done yet?"

"Bratface," Holly whispered.

Kate nudged her. "Hush."

Liz frowned at them. "Like I said, this is a team effort and I expect total cooperation. Some of you qualified, some didn't. For those who didn't get into the Festival this time, I'm proud of you anyway. You'll have another chance next year, and I expect you to support those who did get in. Help groom their horses, clean tack, and muck stalls . . . and make sure they're where they're supposed to be—on time."

"I don't need a babysitter," Angela said.

"Maybe not," Liz said smoothly. "But I'm sure

you'll perform better with a support group." She pinned Angela with a look. "You're quite right about competing as individuals, but you'll also be representing Timber Ridge. And I'm sure your mother is very proud of you."

"What*ever*," Angela said, shrugging.

There was an embarrassed silence. Beside her, Kate could feel Holly getting ready to slam into Angela for being rude, which would only make things worse. So Kate jabbed Holly with her elbow and changed the subject.

"What about the written test?"

In December when Aunt Bea had been helping Liz choose the team's original four riders, she'd given them a killer quiz that she promised would be worse than anything they'd find on the real thing. Two of the questions had Kate totally stumped. Holly admitted to being baffled by three others, and this was good. It made them study harder and learn even more about horses.

Angela sighed. "That is *so* dumb."

"Yeah, *really* dumb," echoed Kristina.

Ignoring them, Liz said, "The written test will count as part of your final score, so I suggest you hit the books. Now, are there any more questions?"

"Stable management?" Holly said.

Her mother nodded. "You'll be judged on that, too."

Inwardly, Kate groaned. She had no problem with keeping her horse's stall and tack immaculate, but when another rider messed it up on purpose, you didn't stand a chance. At the Hampshire Classic last summer, some-one—probably Angela—had trashed Magician's stall right before the judges came by and Kate lost a bunch of points, which dragged down the team's overall score.

It made no sense.

Why had Angela jeopardized her team's chances when winning the trophy meant so much to Mrs. Dean? Holly said it was because Angela only cared about the individual gold medal. She didn't give a hoot about the riding team.

She hadn't left any clues, either.

Nobody could pin the blame on Angela, no matter what she did. Her mother made sure of that.

* * *

Liz offered to drive Sue home. Her parents ran the ski area, and their lodge was two miles further up the road. On the way, Liz would drop off Robin and Jennifer. Angela had already left with her mother, and Kate assumed that Kristina had gone with them.

"Kate?" Liz said. "Do you need a ride?"

"She's staying over," Holly said.

"I am?"

"Yes, because I just invited you," Holly said. "So you'd better call your dad to let him know."

"I'll do it," Liz said, pulling out her phone. "Ben and I need to make plans for tomorrow's lesson anyway."

Kate shared a conspiratorial look with Holly. They'd bought their parents cooking lessons for Christmas in the hopes of getting them together.

So far, it seemed to be working.

Last week Liz had whipped up an amazing omelet with onions and red peppers and everything, and then Ben had taken her to Boston for a butterfly exhibit. The only glitch was Mrs. Gordon who'd declared loudly that she would love to join the cooking class too.

* * *

After Liz left, Kate and Holly dragged out the hose and filled the horses' water buckets. Kate dropped a couple of small carrots into Tapestry's. The horse loved this game and plunged her nose into the bucket as if she were bobbing for apples at a kids' Halloween party.

"You don't deserve any treats," Kate said, trying to sound angry. "You were a bad girl today."

Messily, Tapestry crunched her carrots and slob-bered juice down the front of Kate's jacket.

"Ugh," Kate said. "But I love you anyway."

She wiped off the glop, kissed Tapestry's nose, and then coiled up the hoses before joining Holly in the feed room.

Bales of hay, five layers deep, reached from floor to ceiling. Wooden shelves held jars of hoof dressing and molasses; an old coffee can bristled with tarnished spoons, dried-up markers, and Popsicle sticks. In the corner, bunches of knotted-up baling twine sprouted from a feed sack. Kate grabbed a scoop and was about to measure grain into color-coded buckets when the barn lights flickered.

She paused and looked up.

Cobwebs, laden with dust, covered a low-wattage light bulb and looped among the rafters. The light was so dim you could barely see what you were doing.

"We'd better hustle," Kate said.

They had eleven horses and three ponies to feed. Their grain ration, vitamins, and supplements were written on a huge whiteboard that hung above the bins. Ragtime got the most and Plug the least, with the other horses at various amounts in between. Kate doubled-checked the list, then dug her scoop into the grain and began doling it out.

Beside her, Holly split a bale of alfalfa and loaded it onto a wheelbarrow. On top, she piled six flakes of sweet-smelling timothy, followed by a generous wedge of grass hay for Marmalade and the ponies. The lights flickered again.

"Flashlights," Kate said. "Where are they?"

"In Mom's office."

During last week's blizzard, the power had cut out. Ten minutes later, so had the barn's generator. Liz had tried—and failed—to get it going, so she'd asked Mrs. Dean for a replacement. But so far the Timber Ridge maintenance crew hadn't gotten around to it.

"I'll get them," Kate said.

"Don't bother," Holly muttered. "I think the batteries are all dead." She piled more flakes onto the wheelbarrow, then pulled out her cell phone. "So is this. I forgot to charge it."

Just then, Kristina emerged from Cody's stall with her saddle and bridle. Kate couldn't be sure, but it looked as if Kristina had been crying. Her face was blotchy; her eyes red and puffy. Maybe Angela hadn't invited her to the dress fitting and had taken Courtney instead.

"Hey, we could use some help," Kate said, pointing toward Holly's overloaded wheelbarrow.

A scowl flashed across Kristina's sharp features.

Kate was surprised to see her. Angela's best friend didn't normally stick around the barn after everyone else had left. With an impatient sigh, Kristina dumped her tack on the ground, then bypassed Holly's wheelbarrow and reached for Kate's grain buckets instead.

Did Kristina know the barn's routine? Had she ever helped with evening feed? Kate couldn't remember. Cautiously, she said, "Okay, the blue one's for Magician, the green is Tapestry's, the red is for Ragtime, and—"

"I know what I'm doing," Kristina snapped. "I've fed horses before." She hooked the three buckets over her arm, then grabbed the orange one.

"That's for Plug," Kate said.

It held barely enough to satisfy a guinea pig, let alone a pony, but that's all Plug was allowed—just a spoonful, nothing more. He got plenty of grass hay, but his grain was severely rationed. Too much, and he'd colic or founder—and both could be fatal.

"Don't mix them up," Holly warned.

Kristina shot her a withering look and stalked off. She dumped Magician's grain into his bucket and was about to feed Tapestry when the lights popped and went out.

4

FOR A FEW SECONDS, Kate didn't dare move. The darkness was so complete it was like being trapped inside a black paper bag. She held up both hands but couldn't see them. Small sounds turned into big ones; her imagination ran wild. That cobweb she'd just seen in the rafters probably had a bazillion spiders ready to jump on her.

Horses stomped and whinnied.

They could smell their food and they wanted it now. They didn't care about the dark. They were used to it. One kicked his stall door which set them all off—stamping their feet like toddlers in a candy store.

"Chill out," Holly yelled. "We're coming."

Kate blinked, then blinked again. It was blacker than pitch, like staring at the backs of your eyelids. She couldn't see Holly and the wheelbarrow, but she could hear its wheels squeaking.

"Kristina?" Kate said. "Where are you?"

No reply.

Maybe she was too scared to speak. Some kids totally freaked out in the dark. Even Kate was having a hard time holding herself together.

"Are you all right?" she called.

Arms outstretched like a sleepwalker, Kate shuffled forward and tried to remember what had been left in the aisle. Had they hung up all the rakes and pitchforks or were they lying in wait to trip her up? What about the muck buckets? Were they empty or still full of manure? Kate's memory had fizzled out, just like the power had. She took another two steps and bumped into Holly.

"Watch out," Holly cried, but too late.

The wheelbarrow tipped over, spilling alfalfa, timothy, and grass hay across the aisle. Except Kate couldn't see it; she could only imagine it—a big muddle and impossible to sort out in the dark. They'd have to go by feel or smell.

"Kristina?" Kate called again. "Where are you?"

"Here," came a small voice.

"Don't move," Kate said.

Slivers of light showed through cracks in the barn

door. Ice? Reflected snow? It certainly wasn't the moon, not with a blizzard raging at full tilt. But maybe, if Kate could get to the door and open it, there'd be enough light for them to see.

It was worth a shot.

Horses whinnied hopefully as Kate inched her way forward. On the left, she heard a bucket rattle. That would be Magician, tucking into his feed. Beyond him, on the same side, was Tapestry. No munching noises came from her bucket. None from Ragtime and Plug across the aisle either. A hand grabbed Kate's arm. She gave a little cry.

"It's me," Kristina said.

Kate felt instantly stupid. "Phew."

"Don't you have a flashlight?"

"No."

"Cell phone?" Kristina said.

Kate pulled it from her pocket, feeling even more stupid. Why hadn't she thought of it before? Her phone didn't have a built-in flashlight, but its display was better than nothing. Holding it up, she could just make out Kristina's face. She'd been crying again.

"Here," Kate said, handing the phone to Kristina. "You finish feeding, and I'll get the door open. It might give us some more light."

"Okay." The voice sounded shaky.

But the big doors refused to slide. Their tracks were jammed with ice, so Kate forced the side door open. Flurries of snow swirled into the barn but didn't provide much light—not enough to see what they were doing, anyway. They'd have to rely on Kate's phone. Like a giant firefly, its intermittent glow floated across the aisle as Kristina fed Tapestry, then Ragtime and Plug.

Okay, that was four horses down, ten more to go. Kate closed the barn door, then linked up with Kristina and took the empty buckets.

"Hold onto me," she said.

"Why?"

"So I don't get lost," Kate said. "You've got the phone, remember?" Kristina was clutching it like a lifeline, and Kate didn't think she'd be willing to give it back.

Kristina sighed. "Okay."

She reached for Kate's arm and held onto it. Her hand trembled. Kate could feel it all the way through her down jacket, fleece hoodie, and long-sleeved shirt. Kristina really was scared. Taking baby steps, they returned to Holly, still trying to sort out the hay.

"It's no good," she said. "I can't tell one from the other."

"Then let's play it safe and feed them all grass hay," Kate said.

Holly gave a little snort. "Magician and Ragtime will complain."

"Too bad," Kate said. "They can have the good stuff tomorrow."

Back in the feed room, Kate told Kristina to hold up the cell phone as she filled five more buckets. Together, they made the rounds then came back for a refill. Once the last batch of horses had been fed, Holly packed the wheelbarrow with grass hay and steered it down the aisle. Kate reclaimed her cell phone and aimed it as best she could while Kristina tossed flakes into each stall. Ragtime dove into his like he was starving.

Kate's phone buzzed.

Startled, she almost dropped it. "Hello?"

"I'll be late back," Liz said. "I'm stuck in a snow-drift, and Mr. Piretti's crew is trying to pull me out." The line crackled. "Are you guys okay?"

"Yes, but we lost power," Kate replied.

"The whole mountain went out," Liz said. "Skiers are stranded on chairlifts, so it's a real mess."

Holly shifted closer. "Is that Mom?"

Kate nodded. "We've fed the horses," she told Liz. "But I can't get the barn door open. It's frozen shut."

There was a pause, and Kate heard voices in the background. Then Liz said, "Brad's on his way with the snowmobile. He'll take you home, and I'll be back as soon as I can."

* * *

The barn got colder and colder. Holly made a nest in the spilled hay, and they piled into it, huddling together for warmth like puppies in a basket. Kristina complained it was itchy, but Kate told her to deal with it. The battery on her phone was slowly dying; pretty soon, it would conk out altogether.

"I want to go home," Kristina moaned.

Holly said, "I've got an idea."

"What?" Kate said. Holly's ideas were usually off the wall, but once in a blue moon, she nailed it.

"Let's make Tapestry lie down and we'll snuggle up to her," Holly said, shivering. "She's nice and warm."

"Yes," Kristina said.

But Kate wasn't too sure. She'd taught Tapestry to lie down on command, and Tapestry was fine if one, maybe two, people cuddled against her. But three was a bit much. What if Tapestry objected and lurched to her feet? In the dark, it would be easy for someone to get hurt, or—

From outside came a gigantic, deep-throated roar. It sounded as if a jumbo jet had just landed in the parking lot. Moments later, the barn door slid open and two powerful beams lit up the aisle. Kate shielded her eyes.

"You guys okay?" Brad said, lumbering toward them.

Holly scrambled to her feet and hauled Kate up with her. "We're fine," she said, shivering. "What about Mom?"

"They're still digging her out." Brad pulled off his wrap-around ski goggles. They looked so high-tech that Kate half expected them to have defrosters and windshield wipers. "Okay, so who's coming with me first?" he said.

Kristina leaped up and practically threw herself at Brad. "Why don't we all come," she said. "You can drop Holly and Kate, and then you can take me home. I'm sure my mother would love to make us some hot chocolate. We could sit by the fire, and—"

"Maybe another time," Brad said.

"Smooth," Holly whispered.

"You go," Kate said to Kristina. "Brad can come back for us later."

"Why?"

"Because he's only got room for one passenger," Kate said. She'd seen Brad's snowmobile before when he rescued her from the Halloween blizzard. Poor guy.

It seemed as if he were always pulling her out of one snowy mess or another, including her disaster on "Nightmare."

"Here," Brad said, handing Kate one of his flashlights. "You'll need this until I get back. Ten minutes, okay?" Then he took Kristina's arm and hurried her toward the door. She had a hard time keeping up.

Holly struck a pose. "Oh, Brad, *darling*. This will be *so* romantic. Just like a sleigh ride in Central Park."

"Not," Kate said, grinning.

With Brad's enormous flashlight, she cruised the aisle and peeked into each stall. The horses were all munching hay—except for Plug. His nose was firmly stuck in his bucket, and he was chewing—not scouring the bottom of the bucket like he always did.

That was odd.

Plug should've finished his grain by now.

Unless—

Red bucket. Orange bucket. Two huge scoops for Ragtime; a tiny teaspoon for Plug. Had Kristina muddled them up? Kate ripped open Plug's door, shoved him to one side, and stuck her hand into his bucket. Her fingers registered an inch of grain.

Far more than he normally got.

In a flash, Kate unclipped Plug's bucket and tossed

it into the aisle. She could almost see the pony looking at it, mournfully, as if his last meal on earth had just disappeared.

And maybe it had.

Too much grain—this much grain—could kill him.

* * *

"I'm going to strangle her," Holly said, stroking Plug's nose while Kate put an ear to his belly.

It was comfortingly noisy—a chorus of rumbles and squeaks as if a marching band were tuning up in there. But that could change to an ominous silence if the grain Plug had guzzled turned into a big problem.

"It wasn't Kristina's fault," Kate said. "It was dark, and she's never fed the horses before."

"That's because she's a lazy bratface."

"No, it's because we've never asked her," Kate said.

She hated defending Kristina, but Angela's best friend had come from a barn where the rich girls did no work. They had grooms who cleaned tack, brushed horses, and mucked out stalls. This was probably the first time Kristina had ever been expected to help, despite what she said about knowing how to feed horses.

Holly opened her mouth, then shut it again. Plug shoved his fuzzy nose into her pocket. "Greedy boy," she said, hugging him and looking at Kate with tears in her eyes. "Will he colic?"

"I don't know, but we need your mom."

"And the vet."

"He'd never get here," Kate said. "Not in this weather." Dr. Fleming lived almost twenty miles away.

"Mom won't get here either," Holly said, "unless Mr. Piretti pulls her out."

While Holly fed Ragtime the grain he should've gotten, Kate tried to reach Liz, but the call wouldn't go through. She was about to try again when the barn door opened and Brad made a second dramatic appearance. Holding the flashlight beneath his chin, he lurched toward them and stretched his mouth into a hideous grin.

"The Abominable Snowman," Holly muttered.

Kate said, "We can't leave."

"Why not?" Brad said, brushing snow off his black mittens. They were the size of boxing gloves, with zippers like railroad tracks and gauntlets that almost reached his elbows.

"Because we think the pony's going to colic," Holly said. She wrapped her arms around Plug's neck as if by hugging him she could somehow protect him. He closed his eyes and looked terminally cute.

Maggie Dana

Brad shrugged. "That's a tummy ache, right?"

"Yes," Kate said. "But—"

"So what's the big deal?"

She tried to explain. Brad knew next to nothing about horses, except what he'd learned from his sister and a few riding lessons with Liz. "Plug got Ragtime's feed by mistake," Kate said, searching for an analogy that Brad would understand. "It's like a toddler eating two dozen Big Macs."

"Yum," he said.

Fists raised, Holly lunged at him. "That is so *not* funny."

"Okay," Brad said, fending her off. "So why did he eat it all?"

"Because horses are totally dumb about food," Kate said as patiently as she could. "They pig out till it's all gone."

"Wouldn't he just throw up?"

"A horse can't barf," Holly said. "His gut's a one-way street."

It finally seemed to sink in. Brad's expression changed from goofy to serious. "What can I do to help?"

"Get Mom here," Holly said, "and fast."

5

AFTER BRAD TOOK OFF, Holly and Kate made a fuss of Plug. They found his favorite tickly spots and rubbed them until he curled his upper lip in delight.

"If he's going to colic," Holly said, "I think it'll take at least twelve hours to show up. Maybe longer. What time is it now?"

Kate checked her phone. "Seven thirty."

"Okay, so tomorrow morning."

Until then, there was nothing they could do except keep an eye on him. If he started biting his flank, pawing the ground, or trying to lie down, they'd have to keep him moving. He wasn't allowed anything more to eat, either.

"What about water?" Kate said, peering into Plug's

bucket. It was half full, so he'd obviously had some before scarfing up Ragtime's grain.

"No," Holly said, about to unclip the bucket.

Kate stopped her. "Leave it. I think water's okay. It probably helps flush the grain through his system."

"You sure?"

"No."

Holly finished unclipping the bucket and set it down in the aisle. "Better safe than sorry."

"What about mineral oil?" Kate said. "Isn't that supposed to help?"

"Only if you know how to give it properly," Holly said, "like the vet does."

"Or your mother," Kate said.

She tried Liz's number again, but all she got was static. Before leaving, Brad had warned them that the storm was getting worse. Even he was having trouble blasting through it with his snowmobile. Trees had fallen on power lines, and he'd almost gotten stuck in a snowdrift on his way back from dropping Kristina.

Holly shivered. "I'm cold."

"Me too," Kate said. She gave Holly the phone and reached for Brad's flashlight. It was so big and sturdy that it sat on the ground without tipping over. "I'll get some blankets. What else?"

"Painkillers," Holly said.

"For you?"

"No, silly. For Plug. He'll probably need them."

A howling wind whipped around the barn, shaking windows and rattling doors. Something on the roof shifted, like a giant was up there stomping around in the ice and snow.

Kate ran for the tack room.

Did they have any Banamine? It was the best painkiller for colic, and it would be just their rotten luck to have run out. But no, there it was, on the top shelf, propped up between two bottles of mineral oil. Kate put them in a bucket, then found a digital thermometer and added that as well. She crossed her fingers that Plug wouldn't need any of this, but it was best to have stuff ready for Liz—just in case.

Okay, now for the blankets. She grabbed two of the cleanest she could find and rustled up a nylon stall guard so they'd be able to keep Plug's door open and watch him from the aisle. They could snuggle up in the hay nest, and—

"Hurry up!" Holly yelled, sounding close to panic.

"Is it Plug?"

"No," Holly said. "Your stupid phone just died."

Kate shifted her load to one arm and snatched up

the barn phone. It was hard-wired to the wall beside the tack room door. Hoping for a dial tone, she jiggled the hook, but that line was dead, too.

*   *   *

An hour passed, then another, but there was no comforting roar from Brad's snowmobile. Kate turned the flashlight down to save battery power. Who knew how long it would last?

They took turns keeping an eye on Plug. One watched while the other slept . . . or tried to. Kate was so cold, she couldn't feel her fingers any more. From beneath a pile of blankets Holly moaned.

"I'm freezing. Let's get Tapestry."

Stiffly, Kate got to her feet. She peeked into Plug's stall. The pony was just standing there, head down and half asleep, showing no signs of distress. Across the aisle, Tapestry was dozing, too. Kate clipped a lead rope to her halter.

"C'mon, girl. You've got a job to do." She led Tapestry into the aisle and pointed to her left shoulder. "Down."

With an elongated sigh, Tapestry obeyed. Her forelegs buckled and then her hindquarters as she settled herself into a heap amid the hay.

"She's loving this," Holly said, watching Tapestry nibble bits of dried clover. "It's like a midnight feast."

"How I wish," Kate said. She'd been too cold and too worried about Plug to think about food, but now realized she was absolutely starving. Wrapping herself in a blanket, she joined Holly on the ground and snuggled against Tapestry.

* * *

Something woke Kate from a deep sleep. Disoriented, she sat up feeling dizzy. From inside Plug's stall, Brad's flashlight cast a low beam, and Kate could just make out Holly, leaning against the pony with her ear to his belly.

"Can you hear anything?" Kate said.

Holly straightened. "Nothing."

Doing her best not to disturb Tapestry, Kate stood up and limped into Plug's stall. The pony's eyes were dull; he'd begun to sweat. With a grunt, he turned and nipped at his flank.

"Poor Plug," Holly wailed. "I feel awful."

"I bet he does, too," Kate said. She clipped a lead rope to the pony's faded green halter. "I'll walk him for a bit."

Holly wiped her eyes. "He's going to die."

"No, he's not," Kate said.

"How do you know?"

"Because we won't let him," Kate said, sounding way more confident than she felt. Judging by the faint light coming through Plug's frost-covered window it had to be about six thirty, maybe even seven o'clock— just over twelve hours since he'd eaten all that grain. She had a mental picture of it, stuck inside Plug's belly like a giant wad of chewing gum.

In the aisle, Tapestry lurched to her feet and shook herself. Slowly, the other horses woke up and demanded food. Ragtime banged on his door; Magician neighed and rattled his bucket. Within seconds, the barn was in an uproar. The pony looked as if he wanted to cover his ears.

"I'll take Plug to the arena while you feed," Kate said. It wouldn't be fair to let him watch the others tucking into breakfast. Slowly, she walked him in circles, stopping every couple of minutes to let him rest. But each time she did, Plug tried to lie down. She didn't dare let him.

What if he rolled and twisted a gut?

Kate had read horror stories about that happening to horses with colic. She'd also heard that it was okay to let a horse lie down as long as it didn't roll and thrash about.

But how would she stop him?

Plug was only twelve hands, but he had to weigh at least five hundred pounds. Kate couldn't exactly pick him up like she could a puppy or a kitten.

Head down, the pony dragged his feet through the tanbark, barely able to move. If Liz or the vet didn't get here soon, Kate was afraid they would lose him. A horse at her old barn had gorged on sweet feed and died. She began to cry. Great big tears rolled down her face, and she didn't attempt to wipe them off.

* * *

After what felt like three hours but was probably less than thirty minutes, Kate heard voices. Was that Holly talking to the horses, or was she—?

"Kate," Liz called out.

She ran across the arena and Kate had never been so pleased to see anyone in her life. She wanted to throw herself into Liz's arms and never let go.

"I'm sorry I wasn't here," Liz said, giving Kate a quick hug. "The crews are having trouble clearing the roads, but Brad finally managed to get through with the snowmobile. He's helping Holly muck stalls."

"What time is it?"

Liz checked her watch. "Almost eight."

"Uh, oh," Kate said, yawning. "What about school?"

"Closed," Liz said.

Expertly, she ran her hands down Plug's forelegs and cupped them around his tiny hooves. "They're nice and cool," she said, with a sigh of relief. "If he were going to founder, he'd have done it already."

Kate hadn't even thought of that. She'd been so focused on Plug's belly, she'd forgotten all about his feet. They were smooth and healthy looking, not all wrinkled up like they would be with if he'd foundered and gotten laminitis from gorging on Ragtime's grain.

"Is the vet coming?" she said.

"He'll be here in twenty minutes," Liz replied. "But I'll give Plug some Banamine right now." She pulled out the plastic tube Kate had left in the bucket outside Plug's stall. "Get his head in the air, okay? We have to make sure he doesn't spit it out."

Almost as if the pony knew this would help, he didn't object when Kate held up his nose so that Liz could squirt the medicine into the side of his mouth. He chewed and swallowed. It probably tasted awful, like when you bite into an aspirin by mistake. Kate half expected Plug to pull a face, the way she did whenever she had to take cough medicine.

"Is he going to be okay?" she said.

"Don't know," Liz said. "But he's a tough little guy, and—" She gave a loud sniff and laid an arm across

Kate's shoulders. "You kids have been great. I'm so proud of you. Holly told me what happened with the feed, but I want to hear your version."

So Kate gave it to her.

"It was *my* fault," she said. "I should've fed the horses myself. Kristina didn't—"

"Stop right there," Liz said. "You always do this."

"Do what?"

"Take the blame."

"But—" Kate started.

Liz cut her off. "If anyone's to blame, it's me," she said as they led Plug toward the barn. "I'm the one who didn't buy spare batteries for the flashlights and didn't nag the maintenance department hard enough to get that generator replaced."

Kate bit her lip.

It wasn't Liz's fault about the generator or the batteries; it was Mrs. Dean's. She was in charge of everything that went on at Timber Ridge, right down to ordering paper towels for the barn's tiny restroom and insisting they use her favorite brand of soap that smelled like pickled fish.

* * *

The lights flickered and came back on as they waited for the vet to arrive. Holly walked Plug along the aisle while Kate began to strip his stall. Every few minutes she yawned and stretched.

"Want some help?" Brad said.

Kate handed him a shovel. "Thanks."

The job took no time at all. Brad shoveled up the soiled bedding faster than a backhoe, filling muck buckets that he hauled away as if they weighed no more than a child's basket of Easter eggs. After the last trip, he returned with a bale of fresh shavings.

"All of it?" he said, slitting the bag.

"Yeah," Kate said.

It was kind of fun having a guy hang around the barn. Brad could shred the half-pipe like an expert, but he was a rank beginner when it came to horses. He'd just started taking lessons on Marmalade—the only horse at Timber Ridge big enough to hold him.

Holly insisted that Brad was learning to ride because of Kate, but that was crazy talk. He just liked horses, that was all. You could tell by the way he looked at Plug, who was shuffling toward them with his head down. Brad sniffed and rubbed his eyes.

Was that a tear on his cheek?

Good thing the football team wasn't here to see its star quarterback having a meltdown over a small brown pony.

Wiping tears from her own eyes, Kate was about to

relieve Holly when the vet showed up. He listened to Plug's heart, lungs, and belly with his stethoscope. Liz filled him in about the grain mishap as he took Plug's temperature.

"It's colic, all right," he said.

Kate could barely watch as Dr. Fleming put a tube up the pony's cute little nose—but it was the best way to deliver the mineral oil and medicine that Plug needed.

"Now, you girls keep an eye on him," the vet said, packing his bag. "Call if you need me, and check his stall every hour for manure, okay?"

"I'll take care of that," Liz said. She shepherded Holly and Kate toward the door and told Brad to run them home on his snowmobile. "They're wiped out."

Holly protested, but her mother was firm. "I got five hours of sleep at the Piretti's lodge," she said, "in a real bed, which is what you need right now. No arguments."

Liz hauled open the barn door and Kate could hardly believe her eyes. They had snow in Connecticut, but nothing like this. Snowdrifts, sculpted by the wind, rose like sand dunes in the parking lot. Icicles the size of pitchforks hung from the gutters, and only the tips of the paddock fence showed beneath an ocean of white. The air was so cold that it hurt to breathe.

"This is nothing," Holly said, climbing onto the back of Brad's snowmobile. "You should've seen the blizzard we had four years ago. It buried the high school."

"Yeah," Brad said. "It was great."

"You were still in middle school."

"Wrong," Brad said. "I went straight from kindergarten to tenth grade. I'll be doing my PhD next week."

"Idiot," Holly said.

Laughing, he drove her home first, then came back for Kate. His snowmobile skidded to a stop outside the barn. "Where to?" he yelled above the noise. "Holly's house or yours?"

Pulling on her mittens, Kate hesitated.

She had a history test tomorrow, and if she stayed at Holly's she probably wouldn't get much studying done. On the other hand, it was way more fun at the Chapmans' house than her own. "Holly's house," Kate said, climbing onto the seat behind Brad.

He gunned the engine. "Put your arms around me and hang on tight."

So Kate did. And it felt kind of nice.

6

KATE NEVER MADE IT as far as Holly's bedroom. She flopped onto the living room couch, fully intending to study for her history test, and promptly fell asleep. The next thing she knew, someone was shaking her.

"Wake up, Kate. Wake up."

She bolted upright. "What's wrong?"

"Nothing," Holly said. Tears streamed down her face, but she was waving her phone and grinning like she'd just won the lottery. "Plug's gonna be fine. He just pooped up a storm, and Mom said horse manure has never looked so good."

Kate struggled to her feet. Books, pens, and papers went flying as she and Holly pranced around the coffee table, whooping and hollering and trying not to trip over their feet.

Holly gave Kate a high five. "Score one for Plug."

"And zero for colic," Kate said.

For a brief moment, she felt like a total idiot for getting excited about pony poop, but this was fantastic news—the best, ever.

Kate made a mental note to e-mail Marcia Dean, who was Angela's half-sister and now lived in New York City, with an update about Plug. He'd taught Marcia to ride—along with most of the barn's beginners—and she always asked about him when e-mailing Kate.

Marcia was a great little kid. With luck, they'd be able to see her when they went down to New York for the *Moonlight* premiere. Their tickets had arrived last week, courtesy of Nathan and the film's producer, Giles Ballantine.

Holly was already complaining she had nothing to wear.

* * *

On Saturday Kate insisted she wasn't interested in finding a dress for the Valentine Dance, but Holly put her foot down.

"If you fink out, I'll never speak to you again," she said, folding her arms and glaring at Kate.

They'd just finished mucking stalls, cleaning out

Liz's office, and schooling their horses, and Kate was covered with dirt and sweat. The last thing she wanted to do was try on dumb clothes. Besides, what was the point? She didn't have a date for the dance, never mind that Holly kept saying Brad was going to ask her. And if he did? Would she say yes?

Kate still hadn't figured that one out.

In the end, she had no choice. Jennifer grabbed one arm and Sue grabbed the other as Holly led the way to her mother's van. Robin brought up the rear, just to make sure Kate didn't cut and run back into the barn.

Liz dropped them in the village. "I'll pick you up in an hour."

"Two," Holly said.

The thrift shop bulged with clothes, even more than Kate had seen the last time she was there. The whole point, Jennifer reminded them, was to dress out of character. "We don't want people to know who we are."

"Okay," Holly said, and in no time at all she was sashaying along the narrow aisles like a 1920s flapper in a bright red mini-dress, ankle-strap Mary Janes, and black stockings. In her hand, she held a white pen, twirling it like it was an old-fashioned cigarette holder and pretending to blow smoke.

Even the sour-faced clerk cracked a smile.

Jennifer whipped a long string of pearls from a basket of junk jewelry. "Add these, and you'll totally rock it," she said, draping the fake pearls around Holly's neck.

Hangers rattled as the girls pawed through the racks. Jennifer pulled on red sparkly rights, a red top with even more sparkly bits, and a pale pink tutu. To finish it all off, she donned a pair of heart-shaped sunglasses the size of a Valentine chocolate box lid.

"Funky," Holly said, nodding. "Nobody will know who *you* are."

"Yeah, right," Kate said.

If Jennifer wanted to disguise herself, she'd have to wear a huge heart costume, like really get inside it and peek through a tiny hole in the front. There was one propped in the corner, probably from last year's middle school Valentine play.

Clutching an armload of clothes, Sue disappeared into a changing room. Robin took the one beside her. Moments later they emerged, and Kate burst out laughing.

"Copy cat," Sue cried.

Robin grinned. "Bingo."

They'd chosen reverse outfits. Sue had on black pants with red hearts and Robin wore a long red skirt with black hearts scattered all over it.

"Like a deck of cards," Kate said.

From a box on the floor, Holly grabbed a cap covered with red sequins, tucked her hair into it, and said, "Nobody will recognize me now."

Jennifer tossed a slinky red ball gown at Kate. "Nobody will recognize you in this, either."

The dress had spaghetti straps and a slit up one side, and it fitted Kate like a second skin. Kate blushed as she modeled it for the others, clumping up and down in her paddock boots and Aunt Bea's striped socks.

"Epic," Sue said. "The socks nail it."

"Awesome," Robin said.

Holly checked the price tag dangling from Kate's shoulder. "Fifteen bucks," she said. "It's a bargain." Whipping out her cell phone, she took a photo of Kate. "Nathan will love it."

"So will my brother," Sue murmured.

* * *

That night, Kate and Holly joined Sue and Robin at Jennifer's house to make their Valentine masks. Mrs. West was totally cool about the mess, the glitter, and the feathers that floated around her kitchen as if she and the girls had just had a pillow fight.

On sheets of white cardboard, Holly drew five fantastic shapes. Some had angles and swoopy bits; others had curlicues like a Mardi Gras mask. Once Holly had finished, Jennifer and Sue cut them out, and Robin sprayed them with sparkly paint.

Kate kept her distance.

The last time she'd tried to be creative was when they'd made decorations for Holly's birthday party. She'd gotten glitter up her nose, two painful paper cuts, and glue in her hair. Tonight, the others decided it was best for Kate to pretend she was a nurse, dishing out implements and supplies in the operating room.

"Glue gun," Holly said, holding out her hand like a surgeon.

Jennifer frowned. "Red glitter—stat!"

"Sequins," Sue demanded.

"Red or pink?"

"White," Sue said. "No, black."

Ten minutes later, Robin held up the mask festooned with red beads and pink feathers. "Is this okay?"

"It's lovely," Mrs. West said, setting a platter of burritos, refried beans, and guacamole on the table. "Eat up, ladies. You must be starving."

They were halfway through dinner when Sue said, "Um, Kate. What happened with Plug?"

Kate shot a quick look at Holly. They'd decided not to say a word about Kristina muddling up the feed buckets. It was a stupid accident that could've happened to anyone, even them.

"Remember the storm?" Holly said.

Jennifer nodded. "Yeah, it was a doozy."

"Plug colicked that night," Holly said. "But he's all better now"

There was a difficult pause. Sue glanced at Robin, then at Jennifer, like they were all in on something that Kate and Holly didn't know about.

"What?" Kate said.

"Yeah," Holly said. "What's going on?"

Jennifer took a deep breath. "Angela's been telling people it was Kate's fault that Plug got colic."

It was like all the air got sucked out of the room. Kate stared at her friends. She looked from one to the other. Surely they didn't—

"We don't believe it," Robin said, speaking so fast that her words tumbled over themselves.

Sue said, "But other kids do."

"So how does Angela figure this?" Holly said, eyes blazing with fury. "What, exactly, is she saying?"

"Nothing much," Jennifer said. "Just that Kate messed up and made Plug sick."

"She didn't," Holly said. "Angela's best friend did."

Sue gasped. "How?"

"Kristina was at the barn, so we asked her to help

us feed. Then the lights went out, and she couldn't see what she was doing. She fed Ragtime's grain to Plug by mistake."

"Oh, the poor pony," Robin said. "No wonder he colicked."

"Luckily, he's okay," Holly said, clenching her fists, "but Kate's reputation isn't."

Kate sliced into her burrito so hard it almost shot off her plate. This wasn't the first time Angela had caused trouble. She loved spreading false rumors about Kate—that she'd ridden across Mrs. Dean's lawn on Halloween, that she'd plagiarized an English paper, and that she'd cheated at a big horse show last summer.

There were other times, but Kate was too furious to even think about them. Trouble was, most of the kids at school didn't know one end of a horse from the other, and they always believed Angela's vicious lies.

Would Brad?

As if reading Kate's mind, Sue said, "I'll make sure my brother understands, even if I have to beat it into him."

* * *

They finished the masks kind of late, so Holly invited Kate to stay over and they talked for a while. Even though she wouldn't admit it, Kate was totally bummed out over Angela's latest attack, and she was even more bummed at not hearing from Nathan.

"No big deal," she insisted.

But Holly knew better. The minute Kate fell asleep, Holly checked Nathan's Facebook fan page. It was filled with predictable photos of Nathan and Tess lounging beneath palm trees, holding hands at sidewalk cafés, and dancing cheek-to-cheek on a moonlit beach.

Same old, same old.

So Holly switched to YouTube, entered Nathan's name, and wound up with a video of him surfing at Waikiki beach. He was doing pretty well, hanging ten on his board, until a spectacular wave knocked him over.

Whoever held the camera gasped.

It was probably a clutch of fan girls, thrilled to bits at seeing their favorite star in action. A few seconds later, the camera wobbled. Sand, surf, and bare feet fragmented like a kaleidoscope. Somebody yelled. Then a tanned fist appeared, followed by an angry face, and the screen blanked out.

Curious, Holly dug deeper.

Google pulled up a half dozen articles about Nathan Crane's run-in with a surfer dude who accused the movie star of stealing his girlfriend. Threats and harsh words were exchanged. According to one report,

Nathan got a bloody nose and would've gotten even worse if his bodyguard hadn't pulled him away in time.

Bodyguard?

Quickly, Holly closed the window and cleared her browser's memory as if that would prevent Kate from finding it. She rarely looked at Nathan's fan page, let alone searched his name on the web. What she needed was a local boyfriend like Holly had.

Well, not exactly local.

Adam lived three towns over, and he rode for Larchwood Equestrian Center. His horse was super cute—a half-Arabian pinto called Domino—and he was a dynamite jumper. Adam had beaten Holly at the last hunter pace, but Holly had won the Gambler's Choice jumping class on Labor Day weekend, so they were now even in the ribbons race.

Not that it mattered.

When you liked a guy, you just liked him. It wasn't a popularity contest; it was about hanging out together and being totally comfortable, like you were holding hands inside the same woolly mitten.

With a sigh, Holly turned off the light. But she couldn't stop thinking about Nathan. He'd shown up at the barn last summer because the movie producer, Giles Ballantine, had chosen Timber Ridge to film a scene from *Moonlight*. Adam and Kate had been hired to ride as stunt doubles for the movie's two stars—Tess O'Donnell and Nathan Crane.

Kate hadn't recognized him.

Not surprising, really, given that Kate had zero interest in films and movie stars. But how could you *not* recognize Nathan Crane? He was the most famous heartthrob since Elvis Presley made their grandmothers swoon, like a bazillion years ago.

Is that how Kate felt about Nathan?

Holly had no idea. Kate kept her feelings buttoned up so tight that nobody knew what they were—not even Kate herself.

THIS TIME, KATE DECIDED, she would *not* let Angela get away with it. For once, she'd fight back. But getting Angela on her own, away from Kristina who hovered about like a guardian angel, was next to impossible.

Like right now.

It was Sunday afternoon, and Kristina was following Angela into the arena. She rode so close that Cody almost stepped on Ragtime's heels. Maybe after their lesson Holly could hijack Kristina while Kate cornered Angela in the tack room or Ragtime's stall. It wouldn't take long to give Angela a piece of her mind.

Keeping out of Angela's way, Kate trotted Tapestry along the rail. Schooling inside wasn't nearly as much fun as riding in the outside ring. For one thing, it was kind of crowded, with the whole team practicing at once; for another, snow kept sliding off the arena's roof and spooking the horses. Even Magician freaked out. So did Tapestry. She bounced about like a jack-in-the-box.

"Listen up," Liz said. "You're in charge, not the horses. It's your job to make them pay attention."

Sitting deep in the saddle, Kate used her hands and legs. She pushed Tapestry forward, onto the bit. It took a while, but Tapestry finally got the message. Ears pricked, she swung into a working trot behind Kristina and Cody.

"Good," Liz said. "That's much better."

After a few warm-up exercises, she had the girls riding in circles without stirrups and trotting over a line of cavalettis. Angela complained that they were kindergarten jumps.

"They're not jumps," Liz explained. "They're low poles that help your horse find his balance, and—"

Angela cut her off. "Ragtime doesn't need this."

"All horses need it," Liz said. "The Olympic riders use cavalettis, so don't argue."

Angela kicked Ragtime so hard he cantered over the cavelettis, missed a turn, and catapulted over the cross-rail as well. She almost fell off.

"Serves her right," Holly muttered.

Another chunk of snow slid off the roof and surprised everyone, even Liz. She said, "This is good. It means things are melting."

"Mom's dreaming," Holly said to Kate, waiting their turn to jump the course her mother had set up. "This is Vermont, remember? We're frozen solid until Easter."

That's when the Festival of Horses would take place in Connecticut at a brand new complex Long River Horse Park. It had New England's largest indoor arena, three outside rings, a polo field, four huge barns with stabling for well over a hundred horses, and a two-mile cross-country course that Kate had heard was beyond awesome.

With luck, they'd get to compete on it. But the officials said they wouldn't make that decision until show time—it all depended on the weather.

Liz said not to get too hopeful.

But Kate knew Connecticut. It's where she'd grown up. Two years ago she'd worn a bathing suit and gone to the beach during Spring vacation. Then again, last April she'd been shoveling snow. An old Yankee saying crossed her mind: *If you don't like New England weather, wait a few minutes.*

Maybe this year it would be warm enough to ride outside. The course at Long River was divided into three levels—the easy novice course had fences no higher than two and a half feet, then the intermediate with fences at just over three feet, and a really tough course for the advanced riders.

Kate had seen pictures.

One of the worst obstacles was a rustic fence on a steep downhill bank, leading into a pond with a jump shaped like a fish, followed by a sharp turn and another bank the horses had to scramble up, only to face a coffin jump at the top.

Beyond that was the Tiger's Trap.

Just thinking about it twisted Kate's insides like someone was stirring them with a fork. Good thing these fences weren't part of the novice course, which is what the Timber Ridge riders would be jumping.

* * *

After their lesson, Kate rubbed Tapestry down and waited for the barn to clear out. She wanted to catch Angela on her own without anyone else around . . . well, except for Holly, of course. Her moment arrived when Liz called Kristina into her office and shut the door.

Holly said, "Are you ready?"

"Yes," Kate said. "Cover for me?"

"You bet." There was a pause. "Don't whimp out this time, okay?"

"I promise," Kate replied.

Easier said than done. Kate hated confrontation. She had no trouble when it came to holding her own with strangers, but with people she knew—even the ones she didn't like—she'd fizzle out like a spent candle if things turned nasty.

Well, not this time.

Heart thumping like sneakers in a dryer, Kate crossed the aisle. Angela was still in Ragtime's stall, pretending to groom him, like she had any idea how. At every third brush stroke, she stepped back and wiped dust off her breeches, pulling a face and coughing as if she were choking.

"What do *you* want?" she said.

"I didn't mess up Plug's bucket," Kate said, punching out her words before they dried up. "Kristina did, but it wasn't her fault. It was dark, and—"

"Liar," Angela said. "You're a horse killer."

Memories of Kate's old barn in Connecticut rammed into her like a bulldozer. From far away, she heard Mrs. Mueller's harsh voice accusing her of Black Magic's death. But it wasn't Kate who'd neglected to latch his stall door; it was another girl who was too scared to come forward and admit the truth. For three months, Kate had taken the blame and had even believed herself responsible for the horse getting out and overdosing on sweet feed.

"No," Kate croaked out. "I didn't do it."

But her words bounced off Angela like bug spray off a cockroach. "You did," she said. "And everyone knows it." There was an ominous pause. "You killed Black Magic, and you almost killed poor little Plug."

"Not true," Kate said.

This was spiraling out of control, and right now Angela had the upper hand. Pushing past Kate, she marched into the aisle and whipped around, eyes blazing with triumph. "You're not a *real* team member, Kate McGregor, even if you pretend to be."

Kate opened her mouth, then shut it again because Angela was right. Kate *wasn't* a team member. Right before the December show, Mrs. Dean had invoked an archaic rule that only residents of Timber Ridge could ride for the team. Kate lived in the village; therefore, she didn't qualify. From now on, she could only compete as an individual, not as part of the Timber Ridge team.

"You're not one of *us*," Angela said, her words cutting into Kate like ice picks. "You don't belong here because you can't afford to live at Timber Ridge."

"That's none of your business."

"Oh, yes, it is," Angela said. "My mother will make sure of that."

* * *

From inside the feed room, Holly glanced toward her mother's door, still firmly shut with Kristina on the other side. *Was Mom reaming her out about Angela's vicious rumors?* Holly held her breath and listened hard, but all she could hear was Angela's voice, muffled and angry, from further down the aisle. She could barely hear Kate at all.

That wasn't right. Kate should be shouting by now.

Grimly, Holly began to measure out the grain. Just dumping a spoonful into Plug's orange bucket turned her heart inside out. They'd come so close to losing him. Angela's voice rose again, and this time Holly caught fragments—a few words here and there—just enough to figure out the gist.

"*. . . not one of us . . . you don't belong . . .*"

Angela hoarded grudges like a squirrel hoarded nuts except *she* never forgot where she put them. This garbage was old news. Angela had been spouting it ever since Kate arrived at Timber Ridge last summer.

But it made no sense.

Kate's riding wasn't a threat to Angela any more, not since Ragtime showed up. He was so amazingly cool that nobody could beat him. He'd win for sure at the Festival, and he'd get noticed by scouts from the United States Equestrian Federation—which is what Mrs. Dean was counting on.

Then came Angela's last words.

"My mother will make sure of that."

Choking back her anger, Holly realized that Angela wasn't lying. Kate's father was renting his sister's cottage in the village—complete with an adorable cat named Persy—but the lease would be up at the end of April, so they'd have to move.

But where to?

Ben McGregor had sunk all his money into the butterfly museum, so his options were limited. Even if he could afford a house at Timber Ridge, Mrs. Dean would order the Homeowners' Association to block the sale and make it look legitimate.

No, the only way to get Kate at Timber Ridge permanently was for Holly's mom to marry Kate's dad. Holly had watched *The Parent Trap* enough times to convince herself that she and Kate could pull it off— just the way those clever twin sisters had.

It wasn't pie-in-the-sky, either.

Mom and Ben had already gone on a couple of dates, and they really liked each other. They were taking cooking lessons together, and in April they'd all be going to the *Moonlight* premiere and staying in New York . . . in a fancy hotel with a limousine and everything because the movie's producer, Giles Ballantine, had already arranged it.

It could work, it really could.

For a few magical moments, Holly forgot about Angela Dean and focused on a June wedding—Mom wearing a simple white gown and carrying a bouquet; Kate's father decked out in white tie and tails, waiting beneath an arbor dripping with yellow roses.

Holly and Kate would be bridesmaids in lavender dresses with white daisies and pink rosebuds in their hair; Aunt Bea would give the bride and groom to each other. They'd all throw confetti, and the grownups would toast the happy couple with sparkling champagne. Then Kate and her dad would move into the Chapmans' house, and—

Except it wasn't *their* house. It belonged to Timber Ridge, and it came with Mom's job.

In a flash, Holly's fantasy collapsed. If Kate and her father moved in, Mrs. Dean would play the villain and find a way to kick them out.

All of them.

8

KATE WAS HIDING in Tapestry's stall, hugging her mare and feeling like a loser when Holly charged in. Whipping off her baseball hat, she skewered Kate with a look.

"What did you say?" she demanded.

Kate felt herself shrivel. Having your best friend pounce right after you'd just lost a battle with Angela was like rubbing a sunburn with sandpaper.

"Enough," Kate said. "Angela got the message."

"Are you sure?"

"Yes," Kate said, not sure at all.

She'd said what needed to be said, but Angela never listened. No matter what you told her or how you told her, she'd twist your words into something you didn't mean. She believed what she wanted to believe.

Holly gave an exasperated sigh. "You always do this."

"Do what?"

"Fink out at the last minute."

"I didn't."

"Yeah, right," Holly said. "You wouldn't even stand up to a mouse if it ran off with your last piece of cheese."

Kate gritted her teeth. They'd had this argument before. Holly was always pushing Kate to stand up for herself, but Kate shrank from confrontation because she was seriously bad at it.

Holly wasn't. After her accident, she spent two years in a wheelchair, facing down the bullies at school who poked fun because she couldn't keep up. They'd called her all sorts of ugly names, but their hurtful words rolled off Holly's back the way Kate's words had rolled off Angela's.

Was it all about confidence?

Kate's was a bit shaky at times, but Holly had a boatload of it. She believed she could do anything, and she did. She'd thumbed her nose at the doctors and proved them wrong by walking—and riding her horse again—and zooming right back to the top in junior riders. In April, Kate reckoned, Holly would give Angela a run for her money at the Festival of Horses.

The barn door slid open.

"Brad's here," Holly said. "If you won't talk to me, go and talk to him."

"No way," Kate said, rubbing her eyes. They felt raw and swollen, her face felt hotter than a microwaved pudding.

"Hi," Brad said.

"Hey," Holly said back.

With a cheerful smile, Brad grabbed a pitchfork and began mucking out Marmalade's stall. The big chestnut gelding was easy to work around. He didn't spook over rakes, brooms, and wheelbarrows. He just twitched his ears and gave you a soulful look as if to say, *I'm grateful for the attention, and while you're at it, could I please have a little more hay?*

"Thanks, Brad, I appreciate the help," Liz said, checking each horse as she walked down the aisle. She stopped at Tapestry's stall. "Kate, do you need a ride home?"

"Dad's coming to get me," Kate said.

But only if he remembered. He was doing inventory control at the museum with Mrs. Gordon and would probably forget her. She made a mental note to call him. But before that, she had to help Holly with evening feed. It was almost time, and the horses were getting restless.

"Don't be late home," Liz said to Holly. "You've got homework."

"Looks like you do, too," Kate said.

Papers, folders, and a laptop bulged from Liz's messenger bag. "The barn's accounts," she said, with a grimace. "They're overdue, and Mrs. Dean's waiting for them."

Shifting her bag from one shoulder to the other, Liz headed toward the main door. Behind her trailed Kristina looking sulkier than usual, but her face lit up the moment she saw Brad.

"Oh, hi," she said, her voice a breathy whisper. "I didn't know *you* were here."

With a coy look at Brad, Kristina sashayed into Cody's stall and made a big production out of hugging him. A moment later, Angela joined her. They began whispering and giggling immediately.

Holly grabbed Kate's arm. "You'd better get over there."

"Why?"

"Because if you don't, Angela will get Kristina to ask Brad to the dance."

"Don't be an idiot," Kate said, twitching free. Brad wasn't interested in Kristina, even if he did jerk his sister's chain by pretending to like the cheerleaders.

"Just shut up and go."

"No," Kate said.

"Why not?"

"Because if I do, Nathan will call."

Holly hooted with laughter. "What, you're psychic now? Nathan's not gonna call," she said. "Just because he rang a couple of times when you were talking to Brad, doesn't mean—"

"Oh, all right," Kate grumbled.

The only way to keep Holly quiet was for Kate to walk casually across the aisle as if she'd just thought of something she needed to say.

Like what?

Shoving her hands in both pockets, Kate leaned in Marmalade's doorway and pretended to be cool like the popular kids at school did. The giggles and whispers from Cody's stall grew louder.

Brad didn't seem to notice. He shoved Marmalade to one side and scooped up a pile of soiled bedding. "So," he said, "are you going to the dance?"

"I guess," Kate said.

Just watching Brad toss manure into a muck bucket made her feel better. He'd already become part of the barn crowd, even though he was just a beginner. Kate relaxed. Her silly fight with Holly faded into the background. So did Angela and her stupid rumors. No way would Brad believe them.

He shrugged. "Are you, like, going *with* anyone?"

"Kind of," Kate said, feeling another blush creep up her cheeks. If someone invented a blush blocker—a switch you could flip to turn off the telltale heat—she'd be first in line to buy it. "I'm going with Holly—and the others."

Not exactly true, but close enough. Holly had a date with Adam, and she'd insisted that Kate tag along. But Kate didn't want to be a third wheel, so she'd asked Robin and Jennifer if she could go with them.

"Oh," Brad said, turning red.

A guy who blushed? How cool was that?

He looked away, as if trying to hide his face. This had to be hard, asking her out again she'd pretty much turned him down three times before. Kate wanted to jump in and help him out, but she had the feeling Brad wouldn't appreciate it.

"So, would you—?" His voice was so soft Kate could barely hear him. "I mean, how about if you and I, like, went—?"

This was it.

Behind her, Kate could almost feel Holly leaping up and down with glee in Tapestry's stall. *I told you*, she'd say. *He's asking you to the dance, so you'd . . .*

Someone's cell phone buzzed.

For a moment, Kate refused to believe it was hers.

She kept on looking at Brad, hoping the phone would shut up, but he shrugged and said, "You'd better take it."

"It's probably my dad," Kate said.

Brad nodded. "Yeah."

Reluctantly, Kate pulled out her phone. Without checking caller ID, she said, "Hello?"

"Hi, babe," Nathan said. "It's me."

His voice boomed around the barn, instantly recognizable to anyone under the age of thirty.

Babe?

Blushing even deeper, Kate fumbled for the speakerphone icon. It was like her clumsy hands had just sprouted a pair of extra thumbs. This would be a really good time for the barn floor to split wide open and swallow her whole, or—

Brad said, "I guess that means no."

"No," Kate said. "I mean yes."

"Who, me?" Nathan said, still on speakerphone.

"No, not you," she whispered.

Cupping her phone with both hands, Kate wished desperately that Nathan hadn't called, at least not right now. Despite what Holly said, Nathan really did have a sixth sense about Brad and always called when he was anywhere near Kate.

Where was that stupid button?

Her fingers finally found it, but before she had a chance to mute Nathan's voice, Kristina elbowed her out of the way.

"Oh, Brad," she purred. "I've got a big problem in Cody's stall. Could you—?"

"Sure," he said.

Without meeting Kate's eyes, Brad propped his pitchfork outside Marmalade's stall and followed Kristina into Cody's. The door was halfway shut when Angela stuck her head out. A cascade of black hair fell to her shoulders.

"Tell Nathan I loved his video," she drawled. "I bet he looks really cute with a busted nose."

Video?

What video? Kate stared at her phone as if expecting to see it there, but the screen had gone blank. Had Nathan hung up, or had she cut him off?

Something inside her snapped.

Everything—Angela's vendetta, her argument with Holly, and now this—swelled into a rage Kate had never felt before. It was like being trapped inside a cauldron and unable to climb out.

* * *

Holly cringed. She must've been dreaming to think that Kate wouldn't hear about Nathan's stupid surfing incident in Hawaii. This morning it had exploded all over Twitter and Facebook and gotten even more press than Justin Bieber's latest tattoos.

Cody's stall door slammed shut. Holly could picture Angela and Kristina behind it making a big deal of Brad and inventing stuff for him to do, like pulling cobwebs off the rafters because Kristina was scared of bugs or replacing the clip on Cody's water bucket which anyone with half a brain could do by herself.

Clutching her phone, Kate turned.

Holly had never seen her look so angry. And it was about time, too. Maybe now she'd tear into Angela the way she should have the first time. It wouldn't take Holly but two seconds to lure Brad and Kristina out of the way so Kate could get the job done.

She gave Kate a thumbs-up.

But Kate ignored it. With a face like thunder, she stormed into Tapestry's stall. "It's all *your* fault."

"Huh?"

"You forced me to talk to Brad, and then Nathan called, and—"

"I heard," Holly said. "The whole barn did." She reached for Kate's phone. It wouldn't be the first time she'd shown her how to turn off the speaker. Like Mom, Kate was hopeless when it came to technology. "Here, let me—"

89

"I don't need your help," Kate said, snatching it back. "You've done enough damage already."

"Me?" Holly said.

Kate waved her arms around the stall. "Yes, you. I don't see anyone else in here except my horse, and it's certainly not *her* fault."

"Okay, so what have I done?"

"You've . . . you've . . ."

While Kate groped for words, Holly counted to three. She had no idea what had gotten into Kate, but one of them had to stay rational. There was no sense in both of them losing it. Carefully, she said, "Your anger's bombing the wrong target. Get mad at Angela and Kristina, not at me. I'm your—"

"Best friend?" Kate said.

"Yes."

"Not any more," Kate said.

"What do you mean?"

"I'm tired of you organizing my life," Kate said. "So butt out."

"All right," Holly said, feeling sick to her stomach. "If that's what you want, I will."

9

CLAPPING A HAND over her mouth, Kate stared at Holly in horror. Had she really said those horrible words? Had she just slammed into Holly for no reason at all? If anyone needed proof she was bad at confrontation, this was it.

"I'm sorry," she sputtered.

But Holly wasn't listening. With eyes like ice cubes, she handed Tapestry's lead rope to Kate and walked out of the stall.

"Oh, my," Angela said, as Holly pushed past her. "Trouble in paradise?"

"Big time," Kristina said, grinning.

Kate doubled over. She couldn't remember lunch, but whatever she'd eaten wanted to come back up, like right now.

Yeah, that would be great.

Puking in front of Brad and her two worst enemies? Angela already had her cell phone out, thumbs working like pistons. It would be all over the barn's Facebook page in five seconds.

Guess who just had a fight . . .

Without thinking, Kate turned to Holly for help, the way she always did when stuff like this happened.

But Holly wasn't there.

* * *

Somehow, Kate managed to hold back her tears while Dad drove home. In the front seat, Mrs. Gordon carried on about inventory and stock numbers and how Ben needed to order more pop-up books and butterfly magnets for the gift shop.

He swerved to avoid a snowplow.

Kate tightened her seatbelt. Dad's driving had always alarmed her. He dropped her off, then reminded her about homework before taking Mrs. Gordon home—she couldn't come inside the cottage because she was violently allergic to cats.

This was just fine with Kate.

She found Persy, her aunt's black kitten, washing his paws on the kitchen table amid breakfast dishes and a stick of butter that bore a telltale pattern of tiny teeth marks. He didn't look the least bit guilty.

"Bad boy," Kate scolded.

She tossed out the butter, then scooped up the cat and fled to her room. It reminded her of Holly's—show ribbons around the window, horse posters plastering the walls, and photos of Magician and Tapestry on the dresser, along with Holly's copy of *Moonlight* that Kate still hadn't read. But worst of all were those five tickets for the premiere, now pinned to Kate's corkboard.

She wanted to rip them up.

No way could they go to New York, not with her and Holly—

Kate threw herself on the bed and cried so hard that her tears soaked the pony print comforter that Holly had given her for Christmas. Exhausted, she finally fell asleep . . . and nightmares took over. She was in the barn, shouting at her best friend.

Can't you just shut up and stop telling me that everything I'm doing is wrong? Like who asked you to butt in anyway?

Then . . .

You're jealous because I've got a movie star boyfriend. You want me to ditch Nathan and go out with Brad so I'll have the same sort of plain old boyfriend you do.

An hour later, Kate awoke with a start. Had she really said that, or was it a dream? No, not a dream, a nightmare. For a moment, she lay on her bed and shivered, not daring to move. Beside her, Persy purred like a toy motorboat. Okay, that was good. That was real, which meant her dream wasn't. Downstairs, the kitchen door banged shut. Another good sign.

"Kate," Dad yelled. "Homework?"

"All done," she yelled back.

It wasn't, but right now homework was the least of her problems. The biggest was mending fences with Holly. They'd had fights before, but nothing like this and Kate didn't know how to begin making it all right again—or even if she could.

*   *   *

Kate slept badly, got up late, and barely made it to school on time. The hall was deserted, but taped to her locker with a Valentine sticky was a photo of Nathan sporting a black eye.

Kate ripped it off.

She'd seen it last night, along with the video and a dozen articles that claimed Nathan's fight with a surfer in Hawaii had left him with everything from a bloody nose to a broken arm.

A dumb exaggeration.

Nathan hadn't sounded like he had a broken arm when he called. He sounded, well—kind of different. More grown up, more Hollywood-ish than Kate remembered, especially when he called her *babe*. That was totally gross.

From far off came a familiar giggle.

Angela?

Grabbing her books, Kate galloped down the corridor and skidded into English class two seconds before Ms. Tucker closed the door.

"Glad you could join us," she said.

Oh, great.

Now everyone was looking at her. Kate slumped into her usual seat, but the one beside it was empty. Furtively, she glanced around and saw Holly in the back row. She was the only one *not* looking at Kate.

The lesson droned on, and Kate didn't hear a word. When asked to hand in her essay, she gave Ms. Tucker a blank look and got a stern warning to have it ready by tomorrow or she'd get a D for the course.

What essay?

Had she missed something?

Math, her best subject, was even worse. Mr. Laming's explanation about negative integers went in one ear and out the other, and when he called on Kate to repeat what he'd just said, she came up blank again.

Kids avoided her on their way to the cafeteria. Robin sprinted past without so much as a backward glance and Sue totally ignored her. Of all the Timber Ridge girls, only Jennifer made an effort.

"Do you want sit with me?" she said, choosing vanilla yogurt, diet soda, and a Caesar salad from the cooler.

Behind her, Kate snagged two slices of pizza, a chocolate pudding with lashings of whipped cream, and an extra-large Pepsi. Right now, she needed carbs and sugar. *Lots* of sugar. "Yeah, okay."

Maneuvering around crowded tables, Jennifer led Kate to a deserted table as far as possible from the others. It was close to the restroom door, which gave Kate an escape hatch.

"This okay?" Jennifer said.

Miserably, Kate nodded. "Sure."

Jennifer's heart-shaped earrings flashed on and off like traffic lights as she dug into her salad. "So, what's up with you and Holly?"

"Nothing."

"C'mon," Jennifer said. "Everyone knows you guys had a fight."

Kate shrugged. "I was a total idiot."

"So was Holly."

"How do you figure that?" Kate said. Jennifer wasn't even there.

She took a swig of soda. "It takes two to be an idiot."

"Don't you mean tango?"

"Whatever," Jennifer said.

If nothing else, it made Kate laugh. But inside she was crying. This whole mess was her fault. Holly had only been trying to help. The last time they squabbled, it was Adam who helped Kate realize that Holly was hurting just as bad as she was and that one of them had to make the first move.

"Call her," Jennifer said.

"I can't," Kate said. "She'll hang up."

"So what?" Jennifer said, running a hand through her spiky red hair. "Call her anyway."

But it wouldn't work.

Holly was as stubborn as a mule with the memory of an elephant. She was also the best friend in the world—except when she wasn't—and Kate had the horrible feeling that once you got on the wrong wide of Holly, she could be an even worse enemy than Angela.

* * *

After school, Kate rode the bus to Timber Ridge. Holly wasn't on it. She wasn't at the barn either, so Kate quickly groomed and saddled up Tapestry and headed for the indoor. Sue and Robin were at the far end, schooling their horses, but they kept out of Kate's way.

Overnight, she'd become a pariah.

Except for Jennifer, nobody else had spoken to her or acknowledged her existence. Even Brad pretended she wasn't there. He'd looked right through Kate in the cafeteria, and it hurt far more than she wanted to admit.

Ten minutes later, Liz walked into the arena with an armload of poles. They had small nets on the end like lacrosse sticks. Behind her rode Jennifer, followed by Angela and Kristina. Still no sign of Holly.

Maybe she was sulking, or—

"Gather round, girls," Liz said, waving them into the center of the ring. She handed a stick to each rider. "Has anyone heard of polocrosse?"

Kate had seen videos but decided to keep quiet. Sue and Robin shook their heads; Kristina and Angela were too busy admiring their latest manicures to pay attention. Finally, Jennifer spoke up.

"I played it in Pony Club."

Kate shot her an encouraging look. Jen's dad was a British diplomat. She'd grown up in Australia, South Africa, and England where polocrosse was better known than in the States.

"Good," Liz said. "Tell us about it."

Patting Rebel's handsome chestnut neck, Jennifer explained how the game developed in Australia and spread to the rest of the world. "It's kind of like polo," she said, "but with lacrosse sticks and a rubber ball."

"Quidditch!" Sue exclaimed.

"Close," Liz said, smiling. "Except you'll be riding horses, not broomsticks."

"Do we have to gallop?" Kristina asked, looking anxious. "Like in polo?"

"Walking only, for now," Liz replied. "Or a very slow trot. Nothing faster, okay? You guys are just beginners."

They were practicing passing the ball back and forth, when Holly showed up. Liz handed her a stick, and within moments she took the ball from Angela, then tossed it to Jennifer.

Holly really knew what she was doing.

Kate had no idea. Holly had never mentioned playing polocrosse before. Despite Liz's orders to keep it slow, the game speeded up. Small horses had the advantage, Kate discovered when Sue's fifteen-hand mare turned on a dime and outplayed Magician. He pinned his ears and snorted as if angry that Holly had lost the ball.

"Slow down," Liz yelled.

But Holly ignored her. Stick raised, she galloped down the arena, swerved around Jennifer, and headed toward Kate. For a split second, Kate thought Holly was going to hit her, but she kept going, straight into the barn. Magician's hooves hit the concrete so hard that sparks flew.

* * *

Holly rode Magician right into his stall. It was against Mom's rules, but Holly didn't care. Still holding the polocrosse stick, she flung herself off Magician's back and collapsed. His bedding was none too clean, but she didn't care about that either. So what if her breeches got stained with manure?

Nothing mattered any more.

One stupid fight and her world had fallen apart. There'd be no premiere in New York and no Festival of Horses either. She couldn't ride Tapestry, not after this, and she certainly wasn't going to let Kate ride Magician. He lowered his head and nuzzled her face as if he understood. He hadn't worked up a sweat, so there was no need to walk him out. If she hustled, she could untack him, rub him down, and escape before the others finished with their lesson or whatever it was that Mom had them doing.

"They're getting bored with the indoor," Liz had said that morning. "They want to ride outside, but they can't till the footing gets better."

Holly hadn't been listening. "What?"

"How about polocrosse? We haven't done that in a couple of years. I bet the team would love it."

"Sure, whatever," Holly said.

"We've still got the sticks," Mom said, finishing off her coffee. "Unless rats have chewed the netting."

Holly now looked at hers. It was a bit moth eaten, but nothing a little creative macramé wouldn't fix—if she could be bothered.

Reaching for her stirrup, Holly hauled herself upright and took off Magician's tack. His thick winter coat reminded her of the black bears that lived in the Timber Ridge woods. They were shy creatures and she'd only ever seen one. It was in a huge pine tree, clinging to a branch and looking down as she rode beneath it—a scary moment, but awesome afterward when she got to tell her friends about it.

Friends.

The word got stuck in her throat.

Holly threw on Magician's blanket, fingers trembling as she fastened the buckles. There was no sign of the team coming back, so she risked a quick hug. But not even Magician's warmth could thaw the chill she felt inside or fill the big hole that Kate had left behind.

10

LIKE A MINDLESS ROBOT, Kate went through the motions—classes, homework, and helping dad at the museum, along with riding Tapestry and avoiding Holly. She heard a rumor that Brad was taking Kristina to the dance.

As if she cared.

Her red dress hung in Holly's closet; her mask lay on Holly's dresser—at least, that's where she'd left them. Holly had probably trashed Kate's dress and ripped all the feathers off her mask and thrown it away. Maybe she'd stuck pins in the mask, like a voodoo doll.

She'd probably jinxed Nathan as well. He hadn't called back or answered Kate's texts. According to his fan page, Nathan was now in California. Next up for him and Tess O'Donnell was a multi-city tour to help promote the movie, but it didn't say which cities.

After school on Wednesday, Kate stopped at the feed store. Its bulletin board was crammed with ads for second-hand tack, free kittens, fencing, tractor parts, and anything else you could possibly want along with a few things you probably didn't want, like pet skunks or a tarantula.

Kate shuddered.

Half hidden beneath an ad for firewood, a yellow-ing sign caught her eye: *Free stall in return for barn chores. Call . . .* Kate pulled out her phone and punched in the number, but it was no longer in service.

Last night she'd finally broken down and told Dad she needed to find another barn for Tapestry, like right away.

"Why?" he'd said.

"Because . . ."

It wasn't easy, explaining her stupid fight with Holly, especially to Dad, who didn't understand teenage girls or the concept of best friends.

"You'll get over it," he said. "It's just a tiff."

Tiff?

Was he out of his mind? It was a disaster, the worst thing ever. "I can't stay at Timber Ridge," Kate wailed. "I can't."

"So find another barn."

She'd already called every boarding stable in the local phone book, but nobody had any vacant stalls. One guy said he might have an opening in April, but that didn't do her any good. She needed one right now.

"There aren't any," she said.

"Then maybe you'd better sell the horse."

Kate left the kitchen in tears.

* * *

Kate was still staring at the bulletin board when someone behind her said, "What are you looking for?"

Kate whirled around so fast that she crashed into a cardboard rack. Gardening tools and seed packets spilled across the dusty wooden floor.

"Whoops," the man said.

He wore a denim shirt, cowboy boots, and jeans with striped suspenders. A ten-gallon hat shaded most of a mottled red birthmark on his face, but it didn't hide his friendly smile.

"Mr. Evans," Kate said, scrambling to pick everything up. "What are you doing here?"

Dumb question.

Mr. Evans owned a dairy farm, so of course he'd be at the feed store. He also owned a horse named Pardner that he'd bought at the same auction where Kate found

Tapestry. He'd come to watch her last show, taken a fancy to Aunt Bea, and driven her home in his enormous black Cadillac. It had steer horns on the front.

"Same as you, I guess," he said.

Kate grimaced. "I doubt it."

Mr. Evans plucked a stray pack of carrot seeds off the floor. "I think I'll buy these," he said. "Plant them in my garden for Pardner."

"How is he?" Kate said.

"Ugly as ever," he said, chuckling. "Same as me."

"He's *not* ugly, and neither are you," Kate said vehemently. Pardner might have a homely face with a huge blaze and mismatched eyes, but he had a kind heart, just like Mr. Evans. Without the loan of his horse trailer, she'd never have gotten to the Larchwood show and been able to qualify.

"So what *are* you looking for?" he said.

Kate hesitated. "I, um—I need a stall for Tapestry."

"Like temporary?" he said.

"Permanent."

There was a pause while Mr. Evans hefted a sack of sweet feed over one shoulder. "Let me pay for this," he said, heading for the counter, "and Pardner's carrots. Then we'll talk. I'll buy you a hot chocolate."

"At The Sugar Shack?"

"Where else?" he said, grinning.

Kate's mood brightened. Maybe Mr. Evans knew someone who had a stall for rent.

* * *

Winfield's favorite café had gone all out for Valentine's Day—glittery hearts, red balloons, and bowls of Hershey's kisses in the center of each table. Kate found an empty booth at the back. With luck, nobody would see her. Most of her classmates favored the soda fountain up front. It had swiveling bar stools, free pretzels, and a jukebox that played oldies.

Holly loved it.

Swallowing hard, Kate glanced at the menu. "Hot chocolate with sprinkles and whipped cream," she told the waitress.

Mr. Evans ordered coffee, black, no sugar.

"Spartan," Kate said.

With a chuckle, Mr. Evans patted his ample girth. "Have to keep my girlish figure," he said, then removed his hat and set it down beside him. His birthmark was larger than Kate expected. It curved around one ear and spread across the top of his shiny bald head like a map of Indonesia.

She tried not to stare.

"Now, what's all this about you needing a stall?" he said. "I figured you were doing good at Timber Ridge."

"I was," Kate said, choosing her words carefully. She didn't know Mr. Evans well enough to blurt it all out. "But things have changed. I've looked all over for a stall, but nobody's got anything."

"I do," he said. "I been looking for a horse to keep Pardner company. Poor old guy. He's like me—lives all alone—so having that pretty mare of yours will make him real happy."

Kate could hardly believe her ears. Mr. Evans's four-stall barn was immaculate—gleaming wood, polished brass fittings, and a heated tack room—but it would be way more than she could afford.

"How much?" she whispered.

Mr. Evans laughed. "For you? Nothing. Just give me a hand with the chores now and then, long as it don't interfere with your homework." He took a sip of coffee. "The school bus comes right past my place, so—"

While Kate tried to absorb her good luck, Mr. Evans told her that Bea Parker would be down to visit Holly and Liz that weekend. "I bet you're looking forward to seeing her," he said.

"Aunt Bea?" Kate said.

Holly hadn't mentioned it, but that was hardly surprising. They'd been avoiding one another since Sunday.

"Yeah," he said. "I'm taking her out for a special dinner on Saturday. Got a real nice card for her, too."

Valentine's Day.

Kate wanted to rip those stupid hearts off the wall. Her fingers itched to burst the balloons. Instead, she snatched up a Hershey's kiss and was about to ask how soon Tapestry could move in, when Angela drifted past. Behind her trailed the faithful Kristina. Both girls stopped and stared at Kate, then gaped at Mr. Evans. He smiled at them.

Angela wrinkled her nose.

"Poor Kate," she said, nudging Kristina. "Nobody likes her any more, so she's hanging out with a freak. I mean, seriously. Is that a mask he's wearing, or—?"

But that's as far as she got.

The remains of Kate's hot chocolate went flying as she bolted from her booth and slapped Angela's face so hard that everyone turned to look.

Wide-eyed with shock, Angela clapped a hand to her cheek. "My mother will get you for this, Kate Mc-Gregor. She'll throw you out of the barn."

"Too late," Kate said. "I'm already leaving."

Angela snorted. "Yeah, I bet."

"Oh, but she is," said Mr. Evans. "Kate's bringing her lovely horse to my barn." He held out his hand. "I'm Earl Evans, and you are—?"

"—a very rude young lady," came a familiar voice.

There was a collective gasp as a tall woman in flowing black robes swept up like a Valkyrie. Kate stared at her.

Mrs. Gordon?

"That's quite enough," she said, taking Angela's arm.

Someone gave a small cheer as the crowd parted to let them through. Kate slumped into her booth. All the fight had gone out of her—she felt dirty and ashamed. Her hand stung. Angela's face had to feel even worse.

"I'm sorry," she said to Mr. Evans.

"What for?"

"For hitting Angela—for what she said."

"Don't be sorry," Mr. Evans said. "You can't apologize for what others say. Besides, I'm used to it. I've had this face forever, and—" He gave a wry smile. "Angela, huh? Not much like an angel, is she?"

* * *

Rumors about Kate leaving Timber Ridge spread through the barn like poison ivy.

"She's going back to Connytuck," declared one of the younger kids, brushing Plug so hard that he grunted.

Her best friend sighed. "Connect-A-Cut."

"Wrong," came a voice from the depths of Daisy's stall. "It's Connecticut . . . and Kate's going to be in the movies—with Nathan Crane—in *Hollywood*."

There was an awed silence. "Is that in Connecticut?"

"No, stupid," said another girl. "It's in California." As if for confirmation, she shot a glance at Holly, who shrugged and pretended not to care.

So what if Kate left?

It would make her life easier. She wouldn't have to cringe every time her phone rang or worry about colliding with Kate in the tack room. It was bad enough at school. They shared classes and homeroom, and Kate's locker was right below Holly's.

They'd even swapped combinations.

For a moment, Holly couldn't remember hers. She could only remember Kate's . . . three, one, five.

March fifteenth.

Tapestry's birthday . . . and Kate's, too. Holly had warned her a bazillion times not to use it, but Kate hadn't listened. And now her stupid number was stuck inside Holly's head like a song you hate and can't get rid of.

Ponies clattered down the aisle, dragging excited little girls toward the indoor arena. The oldest, Laura Gardner, had a brand new pony called Soupçon. He'd promptly been nicknamed Soupy, which kind of suited him because he was a deep reddish chestnut that reminded Holly of tomato soup.

Mom appeared in Magician's doorway. "Got a minute?"

"Now?"

"Yes."

"But you've got a lesson," Holly said. "The kids are in the arena."

"They can wait," Mom said.

Knowing it was useless to argue, Holly gave Magician a final flick with her body brush, then followed Mom down to her office. How much did she know? Had she heard about Kate slapping Angela in front of a dozen witnesses, including Mrs. Gordon?

Mom closed the door—always a bad sign—then leaned against it and pinned Holly with a look. "What's up with you and Kate?"

Holly shrugged. "Nothing."

"That's not what I'm hearing."

"Are we having practice today?" Holly said. "Like more polocrosse?"

"Yes, and don't change the subject."

So far Holly had kept quiet about her fight with Kate. The other kids had a pretty good idea of what was going on but they hadn't pushed her to talk about it. Neither had Mom . . . until now.

"I just had a call," Mom said. "From Mrs. Dean."

Uh, oh. That always meant trouble.

"She's told me to throw Kate out of the barn," Mom went on. "But I heard a rumor that she's leaving anyway. So before I hear any more rumors, I want the truth from you, and I want it now."

But before Holly had a chance to begin, there was a knock on the door. Mom opened it half way, and Jennifer stuck her head around.

"Want me to take the class for you?"

"Thanks," Liz said. "I'll be out in ten minutes."

"No worries," Jennifer said, grinning. "That new pony of Laura's is a crackerjack, isn't he?"

"Soupy's a good pony hunter," Liz said. "He'll do well at shows this summer if Laura can keep her mind on riding instead of on boys."

"At her age?" Jennifer said. "She's not even twelve."

"Seems they start young these days."

"I didn't," Holly muttered.

She met Adam when she was fourteen and still in her wheelchair, and it totally blew her away that he wanted to hang out with her. He didn't seem to care that Holly couldn't ride or go dancing or do any of the stuff other girls her age did. He didn't even seem to notice she was paralyzed, and when he did notice, he teased her about it.

And that was perfect.

While the boys at school tiptoed around her like they were scared to talk about it in case they upset her, Adam just charged in. He asked questions and told silly jokes, and best of all he made her laugh.

But she wasn't laughing now.

Mom pulled her into a hug. "I know you're upset, and we'll talk about it later," she said stroking Holly's blond hair. "But for now, tell me how you feel about Kate."

"Why?" Holly said.

"Because I need to know if I should fight Mrs. Dean about this or tell Kate to leave."

"Just because she slapped Angela?"

"Yes."

Holly clenched her fists. She'd wanted to slap Angela a million times in the past, and it was always Kate who stopped her—calm, rational Kate who avoided confrontation. Well, this time she hadn't, and now Mrs. Dean was on the warpath. But if Mom tried to fight her, she'd lose her job. Holly couldn't let that happen, even if it meant throwing her ex–best friend under the bus.

"I don't want Kate McGregor here," Holly said, hating herself, "or her stupid horse."

11

Angela wasted no time blabbing to everyone at school that Kate had attacked her.

"I was just hanging out at The Shack, you know, being friendly," Angela said, "when Kate McGregor jumped out of nowhere and slapped me."

"Why'd she do that?" someone said.

"I dunno." Angela put a hand to her face. "See my bruise?"

"Looks like eye shadow to me," Jennifer said.

Angela sniffed. "It's real."

"Okay, so let's prove it." Jennifer licked her fingers and ran them down Angela's cheek. Half the bruise came off. "You should've used waterproof," she said. "It stays on better."

The cheerleaders glared at her, then circled Angela like mother hens clucking over an injured chick missing its feathers. With a satisfied smile, Jennifer gave Kate a thumbs-up.

"Thanks," Kate whispered.

"So," Jennifer said, as they headed for their next class. "What really happened at The Shack?"

By the time Kate finished explaining, Jennifer's eyebrows had shot up so high that they disappeared beneath her spiky red bangs. "*Go Gorgon*," she said. "Toss Angela in the high school dungeon."

"She can't," Kate said. "She's not the principal any more, remember?"

So far, Mrs. Gordon hadn't said a word, at least nothing that reached Kate's ears. But would she really confront Mrs. Dean about it or just let it go? So much of the trouble Angela caused was buried beneath the rug of her mother's influence.

Jennifer sighed. "Mr. Evans is a nice man, and if I'd been there, I'd have slapped Angela as well."

"How did you know her bruise was fake?" Kate said. "It looked real to me."

"That's because you know zip about makeup," Jennifer said. "And because I never believe anything Angela says." She frowned. "But this time, everyone else does."

"Including Holly?"

"Can't tell," Jennifer said. "She's not talking."

"What about Sue and Robin?" Kate said. They'd both been avoiding her, like they'd taken sides.

Jennifer shrugged. "Sue's mad because you turned on Brad."

"I didn't."

"Yeah, well," Jennifer said. "That's what she thinks, and Robin always goes along with her."

"What about you?"

"I'm cool, for now," Jennifer said, stepping back as a gaggle of kids rushed past, dodging and weaving like basketball players. "But I'll have a big problem if you and Holly don't patch things up."

"Why?"

"Beaumont Park," Jennifer said.

Kate's heart sank. She hadn't even thought that far ahead, but no way could she and Holly go to England this summer if they weren't talking to each other. They couldn't go to the *Moonlight* premiere or the Festival of Horses either.

* * *

That night, Kate's father drove her to Timber Ridge. Except for a single floodlight, the barn was shrouded in darkness. No cars in the parking lot, either. Rolling down her frosty window, Kate checked for footprints in the newly fallen snow, but it was smoother than Angela's lies.

Phew.

She didn't want to run into anyone, least of all Holly, while gathering up her stuff.

Dad parked close to the door. "Need help?"

"Thanks, but I can manage."

Feeling like an intruder, Kate switched on her flashlight and slipped into the barn. Horses whickered as she crept down the aisle. Some were still munching hay; others rattled empty buckets as if hoping she would feed them. This was her first visit since the polocrosse game on Monday, or was it Tuesday?

Kate had lost track.

She aimed her flashlight at Tapestry's stall; to the left stood Magician's. They were the only pair of stalls that didn't have metal bars or a solid wall between them. Magician had his head over the partition, nuzzling Tapestry's mane. She returned the favor by nibbling on his withers.

A lump got stuck in Kate's throat.

Magician and Tapestry were each other's best friends, just like her and Holly.

Kate turned on the overhead lights and slid open Tapestry's door. It squealed, the way it always did.

She'd been meaning to oil its rollers, but that didn't seem to matter any more.

"Hey girl," Kate whispered.

She fed her mare a carrot and gave one to Magician. Then she buried her face in Tapestry's warm neck and wrapped her fingers so tight around Tapestry's mane that the coarse hair bit into her flesh.

Ouch, that hurt.

Kate began to cry. Tapestry gave a soft whicker as if she understood, but Magician grunted at being ignored.

"Sorry," Kate said, patting him.

He'd have to get used to it. Tapestry would be gone for good on Sunday. Maybe Magician would take up with Daisy, his old girlfriend, and Tapestry would have Pardner to hang out with.

But who would Kate have?

Still crying, she stumbled into the tack room, grabbed her grooming box, and pulled her saddle and bridle off their pegs. What else did she need? Her blanket, halter, and lead rope would go with Tapestry in Mr. Evans's trailer. Kate gave the place one last look, then bolted back down the aisle, stopping only to say a tearful goodbye to Plug. She whispered into his cute little ears.

"No more pigging out, okay?"

Dad had opened the trunk. Kate dumped her tack inside and realized her grooming box was half empty—no body brush or curry comb, and only one hoof pick. Where was the other? And what about her sweat scraper? That wasn't there either.

Then she remembered.

She'd borrowed all that stuff from Holly, who'd insisted she could keep it. "I've got extras," she always said.

Well, she'd taken them all back.

* * *

After last period on Friday, Kate slouched toward the gym. From inside she could hear girls with familiar voices arguing over where to hang the balloons.

"On the basketball nets?" Kristina said.

"Yeah, right," came Angela's drawl. "You got a stepladder?"

"No," said Kristina. "But I've got Brad Piretti. He doesn't need a stepladder."

Despite herself, Kate stopped and peeked inside. The gym was like a party shop gone mad—frilly hearts, cherubs with bows and arrows, and enough red glitter to fill a bath tub. Overhead, a disco ball spun lazily among a forest of silver streamers that twisted and twirled like Mobius strips. Kate got dizzy just looking at them.

At one end of the gym, a couple of guys were setting up guitars, amps, and a complicated-looking drum set. Loudspeakers crackled into life; a boy with long brown hair tapped a microphone.

"Testing, testing."

Behind her, someone laughed. "They *always* say that. It's like those are the only words they know."

Startled, Kate turned.

With a grin, Jennifer nodded toward the makeshift band, then shot a glance at Angela and Kristina now arguing over how many helium balloons to put on each table. "If those two clowns ever quit yapping and finish the decorations, it'll be a great dance."

"I guess," Kate said.

Jennifer looked at her. "Sounds like you're not going."

Kate shrugged, then shifted her backpack onto one shoulder and headed for the lockers. The corridor was deserted. Most kids had already left, including Holly.

"Don't you care?" Jennifer said, catching up.

"About what?"

"*Every*thing," Jennifer said. "The barn, your horse,

the Valentine dance." She spun Kate around and made serious eye contact. "Holly?"

"No," Kate said, close to tears. "I don't care about Holly or the stupid dance, and the barn's off limits because—"

"Here," Jennifer said, handing her a crumpled tissue. "Your mascara's about to run."

"I'm not wearing any."

"Yeah, well," Jennifer said. "You should."

Kate blew her nose. She knew Jen was teasing, trying to help take her mind off things. Trouble was, Kate *had* been looking forward to the dance and getting all dressed up. Holly was going to give her another makeover, just like she did for Mrs. Dean's luau and the Labor Day party.

"I'm going skiing tomorrow," Jennifer said. She yanked open her locker and pulled out her hot pink boots trimmed with lime green fur. "Do you want to come with me?"

"I don't have any gear," Kate said.

Or the right clothes, either. The last time she skied, Kate had borrowed a pair of bibs from Sue and gotten a free rental because Sue's father ran the ski area. But now that Sue was mad at her, Kate seriously doubted she'd be getting another freebie.

"No worries," Jennifer said. "We've got tons of extra stuff." She stepped into her psychedelic boots and grinned at Kate. "Our mud room looks like a second-hand ski shop."

"Okay," Kate said. "And thanks."

This sounded like a whole lot more fun than hanging about with nothing to do. Kate flexed her knee. It felt fine, and who cared if she injured it again? There weren't any big horse shows in her future. At this point, there weren't any small ones either.

Besides, spending the day on skis would be a good way to avoid Holly, who'd never learned to ski. But what about the others? Robin and Sue were experts. So was Brad Piretti.

He'd be on the mountain for sure.

* * *

Feeling conspicuous in Jennifer's bright orange parka, Kate kept a wary eye out for Sue and Robin as she skied down the bunny hill. Kids armed with red food coloring had painted lopsided hearts in the snow. Carefully, Kate maneuvered around them. She didn't want to be the arrow that pierced a toddler's artwork.

"Let's go further up," Jennifer said, skidding into a spectacular hockey stop that showered Kate with snow.

She wiped off her goggles. "Okay."

They headed for the gondola. Its rainbow-colored pods reminded Kate of giant Easter eggs. The lift operator wore heart-shaped sunglasses and a red ski hat with two sparkly red hearts bobbing above it. With a cheerful grin, he took their skis, dumped them in the rack, and slid open the gondola door.

Kate followed Jennifer inside.

The last time she'd been in one of these was with Sue and Brad, the day she messed up her knee. It seemed like a lifetime ago.

"To the top?" Jennifer said.

Kate checked her trail map. "How about half way?"

"Sure," Jennifer said, pointing out the window.

Below them, it looked as if Valentine's Day had taken over the mountain. Red balloons tugged at the strings that anchored them to lift towers. A few had broken loose and punctuated the blue sky with bright red dots. Ski instructors wore red mittens and goofy red hats, as did most of their students. And the younger kids tumbled about like gumballs in their candy-colored outfits as they painted even more hearts in the snow.

The gondola clanked to a stop.

Kate and Jennifer got off, retrieved their skis, and set off down a green trail that wound its way gently between stands of trees before spilling into a wide-open meadow. In the middle was the half-pipe.

Leaning on snowboards, kids wearing an odd assortment of clothes hung about like groupies at a rock concert. They ooh'd and aah'd as experts hurled themselves into the air with dazzling maneuvers called "Poptart," "Chicken Salad," and "Bagel." Kate's stomach rumbled. She'd forgotten to eat breakfast.

Brad Piretti took center stage.

His picture-perfect cannonball drew a chorus of whistles and prompted the wannabe kids into giving each other high-fives as if they'd done it themselves. Then a girl with flying brown hair swooped down the half-pipe. Her plaid jacket flapped open as she caught some serious air. At one point she soared so high it looked as if she'd flip herself right over the edge.

"Is that Kristina?" Jennifer said.

Kate raised her goggles. "I think so."

"Wow," Jennifer said. "I didn't know she could do that."

"Neither did I." Kate stepped behind Jennifer so Brad wouldn't see her, not that he'd recognize her in Jennifer's gaudy jacket and oversized goggles. Besides, Brad's attention was totally focused on Kristina. He was slapping her back, and—

"Hey, wait a minute," Jennifer said. "That's not Kristina. It's Gus Underwood."

"Who?"

Jennifer grinned. "That kid who set up the microphone in the gym."

"Testing, testing," Kate said, feeling somehow a little better as she watched Gus Underwood toss back his hair and punch Brad's arm.

"He's kinda cute, isn't he?"

"I guess," Kate said. "Does he ride?"

"Only a snowboard," Jennifer said. "But that's cool, because I'm gonna ask him to teach me."

"Now?"

"Tonight," Jennifer said. "At the dance." She turned toward Kate. "You *are* going to come, aren't you?"

"I don't have a dress."

"You do," Jennifer said. "That red one. I picked it out for you, remember?"

"It's in Holly's closet."

"Big deal," Jennifer said. "Just go over there and get it."

Kate shook her head. She still hadn't made up her mind about the dance.

12

HOLLY'S CELL PHONE RANG as she was stepping into the shower. It was probably Adam. He'd already called three times since she got home from the barn. First he wanted her opinion on what shirt to wear, then he couldn't decide between jeans and black chinos, and finally he'd asked if Holly was expecting him to give her a corsage.

"Idiot," she'd said. "This is a Valentine dance, not a prom."

"Then how about a heart?" Adam said. "I'll bring you a real live one, pumping with blood and a big aorta—"

"Blech," Holly said and hung up.

Still shuddering, she cranked up the hot water. Adam's latest fashion dilemma could wait a few more minutes. Or he'd probably text her. Whatever. She'd deal with it after her shower.

But the call wasn't from Adam.

It was a message from Aunt Bea. Holly had completely forgotten she was coming for the weekend. She should have been here by now. Maybe her cranky old car had finally broken down on the highway, or—

"I'm running late," said Aunt Bea's voice. "I won't have time to stop in before I meet Earl at the restaurant, so I'll see you guys later."

Earl?

Oh, yes, that was Mr. Evans, and Aunt Bea had a dinner date with him tonight. Mom had a dinner date, too.

With Kate's dad.

Wrapped in a towel, Holly sat down hard on her bed. This was exactly what she and Kate had been hoping for—getting their parents together. But now that it seemed to be finally happening, Kate was about to leave the barn, and—

Holly burst into tears.

She hated crying, but she couldn't stop. A river of tears streamed down her face and got all muddled up with the water from her shower. Holly dried herself off, rubbing her skin so hard that it turned bright red.

Great. Now she matched her stupid dress.

Maggie Dana

Angrily, she yanked it from the closet and there was Kate's ball gown, with its tag still attached. Her mask lay on the dresser. Kate hadn't wanted feathers or anything that glittered, but Holly had talked her into it and Kate's mask had turned out better than any of the others, including Holly's.

She ran a hand down Kate's slinky red dress.

Maybe she'd try it on, just to see what it looked like. Moments later, she stood in front of her full-length mirror admiring her reflection as pangs of guilt turned her stomach upside down. This wasn't right.

Or was it?

Holly snatched up Kate's mask. A spray of scarlet feathers curled up one side like an ostrich plume. Fake pearls and tiny rosebuds sparkled amid rows of sequins that came to a point on both cheeks. Holding the mask to her face, Holy peered through the almond-shaped slits she'd cut so carefully just a week ago.

Her eyes glittered with tears.

If Kate were going to the dance, she'd have already come to get her dress, wouldn't she?

* * *

The gym was jumping by the time Holly and Adam arrived. Guitars wailed, drums thumped, and loudspeak-

130

ers boomed as kids with masks and painted faces gyrated to a heavy beat that reverberated off the walls.

With a flourish, Adam pulled Holly onto the dance floor. He wore a Zorro mask and black cape, and he hadn't been kidding about the heart. Pinned to his chest, it pulsed and glowed like Dracula's favorite Halloween ornament.

"Gross," Holly said. "Wrong holiday."

Slowly, Adam opened his cape.

Inside were plastic tubes and batteries and a pouch of something soft and squishy. Holly blanched. It reminded her of the poor frog she'd had to dissect in biology.

"Happy Valentine's Day," Adam whispered.

Holly punched him. "You're a ghoul."

"No, I'm a cardiologist," he said. "I mend broken hearts."

"Yeah, right," Holly said, wanting to rip off Kate's feathery mask. Wearing it was a really dumb move. Ditto the dress. She'd give anything to be able to go home and change.

As if reading her mind, Adam said, "Where's Kate?"

"Sick," Holly said.

He pulled a sad face. "Bummer."

Holly hated herself for lying, but she hadn't told Adam about her fight with Kate or Mrs. Dean evicting her from Timber Ridge. Maybe they'd talk about it later, after the dance was over—unless somebody else got to him first, like Kristina James.

Kristina used to ride at Larchwood and had a big crush on Adam. But that was before she had one on Brad Piretti. He was supposed to be here somewhere, but Holly hadn't seen him. Maybe the rumor about him dating Kristina was a bunch of baloney.

Suddenly, a flash went off, followed by two more. Holly blinked and tried to focus.

"Say cheese," Angela said, snapping another photo. "For the yearbook."

"Go, team," chanted the cheerleaders.

With a coy smile, Angela pointed her iPhone at Channing Alexander. He was the son of Mrs. Dean's best friend, and it was a given that he'd have to date Angela, never mind if he wanted to or not. At the last party, she'd thrown herself into the club's swimming pool to get his attention, but he'd pretty much ignored her. This time he couldn't take his eyes off her. Maybe it was Angela's outfit—a skin-tight mini-dress covered with fringe, sequins, and red feathers.

"The Barbie doll chicken," Jennifer said.

Adam grinned. *"Barbecued?"*

"Southern fried," Jennifer shot back.

Instead of a mask, Jennifer wore heart-shaped sun-glasses and had painted her face with curlicues, silver twists, and big red kisses. Nobody was fooled by her Valentine disguise, including Gus Underwood who dedicated his next song to, *"The girl in a pink tutu."*

Jennifer actually blushed.

As the band swung into Justin Timberlake's "My Love," Holly did a slow dance with Adam. He held her close and whispered sweet nothings about Domino and the latest Larchwood gossip. But Holly tuned him out. She was too busy looking over his shoulder in case Kate appeared.

Okay, suppose she did.

What should Holly do? Stand her ground or run for the exit? Jennifer hadn't said a word about Holly wearing Kate's dress or her mask. Maybe Jennifer didn't notice. It was kind of dark in the gym, and Holly's bargain dress had been red, too . . . just like Kate's.

Would she really show up?

* * *

Kate ran from room to room, flipping on all the lights. Then she gathered up the cat and flopped into Dad's wing chair but immediately got up again. Persy arched his back and flexed his claws as if annoyed Kate that couldn't make up her mind what to do. For the tenth time in as many minutes, she glanced at the clock above Aunt Marion's fireplace.

Nine twenty-seven.

Dad was still out with Liz. He'd taken forever to get dressed and even asked Kate her opinion on three different ties. She'd chosen the navy-and-green stripe because the other two clashed horribly with his pink shirt.

Pink?

Her mother had adored pink, and she'd spent hours trying to convince Kate or Dad to wear it. If only she were here now. First, she'd have hugged Kate and told her it was okay to cry, and then—

Kate gulped.

Mom would've laid into her for slapping Angela, never mind if she deserved it or not. That wasn't the point. Kate had lost her temper and struck out, which wasn't good—especially for a rider.

An old memory whumped into Kate so hard that her legs gave out and she collapsed onto the couch. She saw her mom in jeans and a red-checked shirt. Beside her was a nine-year-old Kate wearing jodhpurs, leather garters, and brown paddock boots. They were at a 4-H show with Webster, Kate's favorite riding-school pony.

He'd gotten loose and wandered over to the next horse trailer and helped himself to a hay net hanging from its side. Kate was about to go and catch him when a girl with huge pink bows on her pigtails came flying out of the trailer. She grabbed Webster's lead rope and smacked him with it, right across his face.

"That's *my* pony's hay," she shrieked.

For a moment, Kate was too stunned to move.

That girl had hit Webster.

A ball of fury exploded inside Kate. She charged at the girl and punched her so hard, she fell over backward. Then Kate wrapped her arms around Webbie's sweet little nose and burst into angry tears.

Mom was there in a flash.

With a firm hand she led Kate back to their car, ordered her still furious daughter into the front seat, and told her that only bullies hit other people.

"Don't use your fists, use your words," Mom said. "They're the most powerful weapon you have." She gave Kate a box of tissues. "Now wipe your eyes and then go on over there and apologize to that little girl for punching her."

"No," Kate said, blowing her nose. "She hit Webbie. She was bad."

"I agree," said Mom. "And you were bad too, for hitting *her*." There was a long pause. "I'm counting on you to do the right thing. I won't force you to apologize, but you've got to think about it, Kate. You can't solve problems with your fists. Solve them with your brain and your words."

Hugging Persy so tight that he squeaked, Kate remembered how it had felt to walk over to that trailer. Each step was pure torture. The little girl, whose name was Emily, was crying as a woman in black boots and breeches scolded her for hitting the pony.

"I'm sorry," Kate blurted. "Really sorry."

"Me, too," sobbed Emily.

The memory faded into a blur, but Kate had a vague recollection of her and Emily hanging out together with their ponies and cheering each other on. They both learned a hard lesson that day, and Kate had never hit anyone else again, until—

A feeling of intense shame washed over her. Tomorrow, she would find Angela and apologize. No, that wouldn't work because Kate would only be at the barn long enough to collect Tapestry, and she doubted Angela would be there that early.

Okay, then she'd do it at school.

But that wouldn't work either. Angela always traveled with the cheerleaders, who swarmed like protective bees around their precious queen. If Kate apologized in front of them, they'd turn it into a mock-fest.

How about e-mail?

Kate reached for her laptop. Did she have Angela's address? Yes, there it was, attached to an old message from Liz about riding team practice. Swallowing hard, Kate began to type:

Dear Angela, I'm really, really sorry for hitting you. I hope your face is better now. Love Kate.

Ugh. That was totally sappy.

Angela, sorry for hitting you. Kate.

That was even worse. Kate thought for a moment, then tried again.

Angela, I'm really sorry for what happened at The Sugar Shack. I should not have slapped you, and I hope you'll accept my apology. Kate.

Before she could change her mind, Kate clicked *send* and was about to close her laptop when a Facebook alert popped up. She checked her own page— nothing new there—so it had to be from the barn.

Pictures of the school dance erupted like lava— Robin and Sue hamming it up in their reverse outfits, Jennifer striking a goofy pose. Then came a shot of Kristina wearing a sparkly red jacket and black tights, followed by one of Adam, looking more like Dracula than a Valentine date with his arm draped casually around Holly's shoulders.

Kate blinked and looked again.

What was Holly doing in *her* dress and *her* mask?

13

Kate shivered as reality ran its cold fingers down her spine. The last rays of hope she'd had about making up with Holly and not having to leave the barn dissolved like ice cubes in a bucket of hot water.

Tomorrow morning at eight Dad would drop her at Mr. Evans's farm. By eight thirty Tapestry would be in his trailer, on the way to her new home. Reluctantly, Kate looked at the clock. Five past ten. She'd been staring at these miserable pictures for half an hour, and she couldn't seem to stop.

It was like probing a sore tooth.

The front doorbell rang. Was that Dad? Had he forgotten his keys again? If so, why not go around the back? It was rarely locked.

Another ring. Longer this time.

Feeling guilty, Kate snapped her laptop shut as if she'd just been caught looking at something she ought not to be looking at like the time she went hunting for her Christmas gifts and found them and then had to fake surprise on Christmas morning.

Kate was a rotten actor.

Mom had figured it out right away but didn't say a word, and Kate never looked for her presents again. With a sigh, she shoved Persy off her lap and wobbled to her feet. She'd been sitting in the same position for so long that her left foot tingled. She hopped to the front door and yanked it open.

"Aunt Bea?" she cried. "What are *you* doing here?"

"I might ask you the same thing," Aunt Bea said, wagging a finger at Kate. Snow had frosted Aunt Bea's knitted hat like a giant woolly cupcake; a quilted bag bristling with needles and balls of yarn hung from her shoulder. "Now, may I come in or are you going to leave me on the porch freezing to death?"

* * *

While Aunt Bea warmed herself by the fire, Kate escaped into the kitchen to make hot chocolate. She measured and stirred and took as long as she dared, knowing it wouldn't stop the inevitable questions—it would only delay them. But it gave her a few extra minutes to think of a plausible reason for not being at the school dance.

Too much homework?

That'd never work.

How about, *I didn't have a date*?

Aunt Bea would see through that in a nanosecond. "I wasn't feeling well," Kate finally said.

"That's the dumbest excuse in the book," Aunt Bea said, reaching for her mug. "Try again."

Kate knew it was hopeless to lie. Aunt Bea wrote mystery novels for a living and could ferret out information faster than an FBI agent. "How did you know I was at home?"

"Clues," replied Aunt Bea.

"Like what?" Kate said.

Aunt Bea tapped her forehead. "One, it's Valentine's Day, and the high school parking lot is jammed with cars; two, I saw your dad and Liz as I was leaving the restaurant; and three, your house is lit up like a crime scene, which told me that even though all the other kids were at the dance, you were home by yourself." She took a sip of hot chocolate. "So are you going to tell me why, or do I have to figure that out as well?"

When Aunt Bea got like this, she reminded Kate of

Ms. Frizzle in *The Magic School Bus*, right down to her corkscrew red curls and oddball clothes. Tonight's ensemble—purple jacket, plaid skirt, and turquoise cowboy boots—would put Jennifer in the shade.

From her quilted bag, Aunt Bea pulled four wooden needles and a ball of fuzzy blue yarn. It had bobbles and beads and tiny silver disks that twinkled like Christmas lights. "I'm waiting."

It all came out in a rush—Kate's ridiculous fight with Holly, being ostracized at school, and slapping Angela in front of Mrs. Gordon.

"Earl told me about that," Aunt Bea said, knitting furiously. "Did you apologize to Angela?"

"Tonight," Kate said. "I e-mailed her."

"Good," said Aunt Bea. "What else?"

"This." Kate opened up her laptop. "That's *my* dress Holly's wearing . . . and *my* mask."

"Hmm," Aunt Bea said, peering at the screen through a pair of wire-rimmed spectacles that kept slipping down her nose. "Seems to me that Holly's sending you a message."

"Yes," Kate said. "She hates me."

"I don't think so," Aunt Bea said. "But I'll find out for sure later." She drained her mug, then packed away her needles and yarn. "Thanks for the hot chocolate."

A ball of blue yarn skittered across the floor. Claws

on full alert, Persy pounced and dragged it beneath the couch.

"Sorry," Kate said, leaping after him.

"Don't worry," Aunt Bea said. "I have plenty more."

As she hauled herself out of Dad's wing chair, a whiff of spicy perfume tickled Kate's nose. Patchouli, maybe? She let out a gigantic sneeze, followed by two more.

"Getting sick?" Aunt Bea said, wrapping herself in a voluminous green cape. If she got caught in a high wind, she'd take off like Mary Poppins.

"I'm fine," Kate choked out.

And she really was. Somehow, things had shifted. Kate wasn't sure how or why, but as she watched Aunt Bea sail out the front door and climb into her car—now dusted with new snow—she felt a faint glimmer of hope.

Mary Poppins?

Holly would've gotten a big charge out of that.

* * *

For once, Adam was speechless. He opened his mouth, then shut it again as Holly blurted out her problems with Kate. But the more she talked about them, the dumber they sounded.

Even dumber was her idiotic fear that Mom would lose her job if she disagreed with Mrs. Dean. They'd been down this road before, and it was always Kate who said they shouldn't do anything that would jeopardize Liz's position at Timber Ridge.

Kate.

She lived less than a block from The Sugar Shack, where Holly now sat in a booth—probably the same one where Kate had sat in when she slapped Angela. She was at the front counter with Kristina and the other cheerleaders, giggling and screaming because Angela had won a prize for the mask she'd paid a fortune for at Blaines.

Holly glanced at Adam, who was still looking like he didn't know what to say, which was kind of odd. Last summer when she and Kate had spent a week avoiding each other, it was Adam who'd talked sense into Kate and convinced her to call Holly.

"Do guys have fights like this?" she said.

"Sure. All the time."

"And?"

"We get over 'em," Adam said, scooping up a generous spoonful of buttercrunch ice cream. He offered it to Holly.

Her favorite. "How?"

"I dunno." He shrugged. "We just do."

"That is so *not* helpful," Holly snapped.

Adam pulled off his heart, still glowing and filled with whatever was inside that pouch he'd shown her. Pond water, probably.

"Here, you need a new one," he said, thrusting it toward her. "So does Kate, but I haven't got another, so you'll have to share this one. It'll do you good."

Closing her eyes, Holly counted to ten. No point in fighting with Adam over this. She already had her hands full with Kate. "Thanks, but you can keep the heart. Save it for next Halloween."

"Call her," Adam whispered.

"What?"

"You heard," he said, sliding out of their booth. "Don't be stubborn. You're worse than a mule."

"Am not."

He held out his hand. "C'mon, I'll drive you home. Maybe Aunt Bea will talk some sense into you."

* * *

From her front door, Holly watched Adam back his truck down the snow-covered driveway. He stuck his head out the window. A puff of wind caught his wavy blond hair and ruffled it. "I'll call you tomorrow," he yelled and blew her a kiss.

She blew one back.

The living room clock chimed and startled her. Eleven thirty. Mom was already in bed and there was no sign of Aunt Bea. Kicking off her Mary Janes, Holly raced into her bedroom. She swapped Kate's red dress for her warmest sweatpants, then scraped off all her make-up. It was like scraping off someone she never wanted to be . . . ever again.

The back door banged open.

Interrogation time.

Dragging her feet like sandbags, Holly dawdled along the hall and sidled into the living room. She straightened pillows that didn't need straightening and lined up her mother's collection of wooden horses on the mantel. That photo of Magician was a bit off kilter. She reached up, and—

"Is that you, Holly?" called Aunt Bea.

"Yes."

"Then come here where I can see you."

Holly shoved both hands in her pockets and slouched into the kitchen. Aunt Bea didn't waste time. She dumped her quilted bag on the table, parked herself in a chair, and patted the one beside it.

"Sit," she commanded.

Holly sat. "Do you want coffee, or—?"

She glanced at her mother's fancy new espresso machine, distressingly empty and way too complicated to figure out. Kate's dad had given it to her for Christmas, and the first time they'd used it, a whole bunch of steam came out and Holly was scared it would blow up.

"Thank you, but Kate made me a delicious mug of hot chocolate," Aunt Bea said. "Now tell me what's going on, young lady. And don't leave anything out."

"Sounds like you've already heard."

"I've heard Kate's side," said Aunt Bea, "and now I want to hear yours."

Knowing it was useless to beat around the bush, Holly plunged in with both feet. She told Aunt Bea about Kate getting mad at her for interfering when all Holly wanted to do was help, and how Kate had told her to butt out.

"So you did?"

Holly nodded.

"Then what?"

"I, er—"

"Go on," said Aunt Bea, "because I think we're getting somewhere."

"Kate slapped Angela."

"Yes, I know," Aunt Bea said. "Earl told me."

"Then Mrs. Dean told Mom to throw Kate out of the barn."

"For slapping Angela."

"Yes," Holly said, close to tears.

"How did Liz handle that?" said Aunt Bea, pinning Holly with a look as if she already suspected something.

"She—" Holly faltered.

Desperately, she looked for something to keep her hands busy, but the only thing within reach was Aunt Bea's knitting bag. She pulled out a ball of fuzzy blue yarn. A dozen stitches fell off one of its needles attached to something Holly couldn't identify. She tried to put them back on again. "Will you teach me to knit?"

"Yes, and don't change the subject."

"Mom asked me how I felt about Kate," Holly mumbled.

"And?"

"I told Mom I hated her, and—" Holly wiped her eyes, but the tears came anyway—great big ones that tasted faintly of salt. Or maybe it was guilt. Aunt Bea gave her a handkerchief the size of a pillowcase. Holly buried her face in it and sneezed.

Patchouli?

"You don't hate her, so why did you lie?" Aunt Bea's voice was so soft that Holly had to lean closer.

"Because of Mom's job," Holly blurted.

Aunt Bea rescued her knitting. "Ah," she said, picking up the stitches that Holly had dropped.

"Sorry."

"Don't be sorry about this," said Aunt Bea, holding up her latest creation. It had floppy legs, or maybe they were ears.

"What is it?"

"An Easter bunny."

"Blue?" Holly said.

"Yes, now keep talking," Aunt Bea said.

Holly took a deep breath. "Mom knew Kate and I had a fight, but—"

"She didn't know the details, right?" Aunt Bea's needles clicked like castanets. "In other words, you guys hadn't had a good talk about it."

Holly hung her head. "No."

"So your mom's flying in the dark over this?"

"Yeah."

"Okay," said Aunt Bea. "Let me try and fill in the blanks here, because if I wait for you, we'll be here all night." She set down her knitting. "One, Mrs. Dean told Liz to evict Kate from the barn for slapping Angela. Two, your mom asked if you wanted Kate to leave, because if you didn't, she'd go to bat for her. Am I right?"

Holly nodded, too choked up to speak.

"Okay, now for number three," Aunt Bea said. "You don't want your mom to argue with Mrs. Dean because you're afraid Mrs. Dean will fire her."

"Yes."

"So you lied to protect Liz's job."

"Yes."

Aunt Bea started counting on her fingers. "How many times have you and Kate done this? Four? Five? And what has your mother always told you?"

Holly felt herself turn red. "That it's her job to worry about her career, not ours."

"And what does this tell you?"

"I, I—" Holly burst into tears again. "I've ruined everything. It's all my fault. Kate's leaving, and there's nothing I can do about it."

"You're right," said Aunt Bea. "Nothing can be done about that—at least, not immediately."

Holly caught her breath. "What do you mean?"

"Earl's really looking forward to having Tapestry in his barn," Aunt Bea said. "So let's not mess with that—for now."

"But, but—"

"We've got Mrs. Dean to deal with, remember?"

Mrs. Dean.

Holly slumped in her chair. Now that Angela's

mother had won, she'd never let Kate back in the barn, no matter what Mom said.

"We're cooked," Holly said, feeling sick.

Aunt Bea shook her head. "Not necessarily. I have a secret weapon."

"Like what?" Holly said.

Aunt Bea *always* had secret weapons, but they belonged in the pages of her mystery novels. Like the characters in a *Midnight* book, they were always too big and too outrageous to fit into real life situations.

"Animal, vegetable, or mineral?" Aunt Bea said.

This was the name of a famous TV game show from before Holly's mom was born, but Aunt Bea had loved it. She insisted it really made you think, not like the silly ones they had today.

"Animal?" Holly said.

Aunt Bea nodded. "Two words."

This usually meant a person rather than an animal with four legs. Holly thought for a minute. Aunt Bea loved sleuths. Her favorites were Nancy Drew, Sherlock Holmes, and James Bond, even though he wasn't really a sleuth.

"James Bond?" Holly finally said. The latest double-oh-seven film had just come out.

"Not this time," said Aunt Bea, as the clock struck midnight. "Cecilly Gordon."

14

KATE'S ALARM RANG at six thirty. Through bleary eyes, she peered at her window. Frost had painted patterns on the glass; curves of fresh snow softened the corners of each pane. It reminded Kate of the bow-fronted shop windows on old-fashioned Christmas cards. All it needed was a romantic couple in Victorian dress, a sprig of holly, and—

Holly.

Was she waking up, too? Was she snuggled beneath her pony-print comforter, trying to ignore her noisy alarm clock? Its thundering hooves had almost airlifted Kate off Holly's spare bed the first time it blasted her awake.

Outside, something rumbled.

Headlights swept across Kate's window and lit up

her room like a carnival. The snowplows were out. They always cleared the village first, then the school parking lots, followed by the ski area, because that was a major tourist attraction. But it took them a while to reach the remote hills where Mr. Evans's farm was. Maybe he wouldn't be able to get Tapestry today.

Kate's heart sank.

She didn't want Tapestry to spend another day at Timber Ridge. The other horses were giving her the cold shoulder. Well, not really, but the kids were certainly giving it to Kate, big time. Nobody, apart from Jennifer, had spoken to her since Sunday. Shunting Persy to one side, Kate sat up and threw off the covers. The cat yawned and promptly curled up on her pillow.

If only she could do that . . . just blow off the entire day and spend it in bed.

Before going downstairs, Kate tucked her blankets around Persy. No doubt he'd be in exactly the same spot when she came home, probably not long from now. There wasn't a lot to do at Mr. Evans's place except muck stalls and groom her horse. With no indoor arena she wouldn't get much riding done until the ground thawed.

Not that it mattered any more.

Maybe her father was right. Maybe she ought to sell Tapestry and find something else to do with her

time, like work with Dad at his butterfly museum
and—

What, exactly?

Her whole life had been wrapped up in horses. She
didn't know how to do anything else. Okay, so how
about volunteering at the local 4-H group or therapeu-
tic riding center? Maybe they'd welcome her help and
Tapestry's, too. The younger kids thought it was really
cool when Kate made Tapestry lie down and they got to
snuggle her.

With a shiver, Kate grabbed her barn clothes and
raced for the bathroom. It was the warmest place in the
house.

* * *

The smell of bacon lured her into the kitchen. Dad was
at the stove looking unexpectedly domestic in a white
butcher's apron. He was also on his iPhone.

This early in the morning?

"Is everything okay at the museum?" Kate said.

Dad really cared about his critters. She did, too, but
it would just be her rotten luck if he were called to the
bedside of a sick moth or a butterfly with broken wings
and couldn't drive her to Mr. Evans's farm.

"Fine, fine," Dad said, dropping his cell phone into
the voluminous pocket of his apron where it would

probably get covered with flour, breadcrumbs, and dried parsley. He reached for a spatula. "One egg or two?"

"Three," Kate said. Last night's dinner had been a Granny Smith apple and two stale Oreo cookies. "Do we have any muffins?"

Looking proud, Dad pointed to a basket on the table covered with a blue-and-white-striped dish towel. Kate lifted one corner. A warm, buttery smell tinged with cloves and cinnamon wafted out.

Yum.

"How long have you been up?"

"Since five," Dad said, cracking eggs with one hand like an expert. He jiggled the frying pan a bit, then abandoned the stove and scooped Kate into a clumsy hug. His beard tickled her face. "This is a tough day for you."

"Yes," she said, gulping.

When Dad got like this, it threw her for a loop. He'd always been cool and reserved and far too immersed in his moths and butterflies to pay much attention to Kate and her riding. But now, after moving to Timber Ridge and meeting Liz, all the all old goalposts had shifted.

So had the cooking lessons.

They'd jump-started his life. Dad was now planning

a Food Network tutorial with Liz—several steps up from the *Cooking for Newbies* course that Kate and Holly had given their parents for Christmas as a way of getting them together.

"I want you to know," Dad said, patting Kate's back, "that Liz feels really bad about this."

"She does?"

"Yes."

The frying pan spattered and claimed Dad's attention, so Kate pulled away. It still wasn't easy for him to talk about feelings. It wasn't easy for her either. They weren't like Sue's family, who yelled and screamed and got in each other's faces one minute, then hugged one another the next without missing a beat.

A month ago—even a week ago—it had all seemed so easy, so straightforward. She and Holly were best friends. They wanted their two lonely parents to get together and form a family.

What could be simpler than that?

But Kate's temper, Holly's stubborn pride, and Angela's lies had blown it all to bits. Everything was a mess—worse than the ball of yarn Persy had pinched last night and totally mangled beneath Aunt Marion's couch.

Aunt Marion.

That was another worry. In early May she would

return from South Carolina, or wherever she was, and reclaim her cottage. Kate and Dad would have to move.

But where to?

*   *   *

Miraculously, the roads had been cleared all the way to Mr. Evans's farm. "Should I come to Timber Ridge with you?" Dad said.

Kate hesitated. "No, best not."

She knew Dad meant well, but he was hopeless around horses. And besides, what could he do except hang about and get in the way? No, this was something she had to handle on her own.

"But you can come and say hello to Pardner," she said.

"Is *that* what you call Mr. Evans?"

"No, that's his horse," Kate said, pointing to a large red sign above the barn door that said, "Pardner's Place."

She'd brought Dad up on Friday night to meet Mr. Evans. They seemed to get along fine, and over a cup of coffee they enjoyed a lively discussion about bugs, especially the ones that plagued Mr. Evans's vegetable garden and bored holes in his heirloom tomatoes.

Kate stepped into the barn.

As usual, nothing was out of place. Rakes, pitchforks, and brooms with red handles hung from brass hooks on the wall. Beneath them, sat a pile of freshly scrubbed red buckets. Even Mr. Evans's wheelbarrow looked as if it had never been used. Not a single shaving or fleck of manure marred its shiny black surface where Max, the barn's inscrutable red tabby, sat washing his paws.

Whickering softly, Pardner stuck his homely head over the stall door. He wore a hand-tooled leather halter with raised stitching and a tiny brass nameplate. Framed by his enormous white blaze, Pardner's mismatched eyes looked hopefully at Kate. She fed the stocky chestnut a couple of carrots, then told him that Mr. Evans would be growing a lot more carrots that summer.

"Just for you," she whispered.

Someone chuckled. "And those pesky bunnies."

"Hi," Kate said, feeling suddenly shy.

Behind Mr. Evans stood her dad, looking as out of place in a barn as Mr. Evans would look in a butterfly museum. Turning away to hide her blush, Kate glanced at the stall beside Pardner's—fresh shavings, a blue bucket filled with fresh water, and sweet smelling timothy in a blue hay net.

Blue?

Everything else in Mr. Evans's barn was red—lead

ropes, muck buckets, broom handles, even the cat. Had he somehow tuned into the fact that Tapestry looked really good in blue?

"That's for your horse," said Mr. Evans.

Kate looked closer. On the door was a blue wooden sign that said simply, *Tapestry*.

She gulped. "Oh, sweet."

"Tell you what," Mr. Evans said. "Why don't I go and get that pretty mare of yours? You just stay here and relax."

"No," Kate said. "I couldn't."

Mr. Evans waved toward his tiny tack room. "There's plenty of magazines in there for you to read, and I just made a jug of hot apple cider. So help yourself."

Something in his voice reminded Kate of Aunt Bea, and it said: *Don't argue. Just do as I tell you.*

"I'll give you a hand," said Kate's father.

Mr. Evans nodded. "That would be fine, Ben."

Without giving Kate a chance to object, Mr. Evans clapped his beefy arm across Dad's shoulders and led him out of the barn, talking a mile a minute about organic pest control and how Monarch butterflies were crucial for crop pollination.

* * *

For a few quiet moments, Kate stared at the empty stall, trying to imagine Tapestry in it. Yes, her name was on the door, there was a blue hay net filled with first-cut timothy, and Pardner was ready to nuzzle her mane the way Magician did.

But was that enough?

For Tapestry, it probably was. But what about Kate? Who would she hang out with? This wasn't a training barn filled with kids who loved horses, it was a working dairy farm. Mr. Evans's prize-winning cows produced gallons of rich milk that Ben & Jerry's bought for their world-famous Vermont ice cream.

Kate was lucky to be here.

Super lucky.

Without Mr. Evans's generosity she'd be advertising Tapestry on horsesforsale.com or posting flyers at the feed store. Feeling like an ungrateful brat, Kate opened the tack room door. A blast of warm air hit her in the face.

Wow!

It was like the western equivalent of Dover Saddlery—gleaming leather, silver bits, and colorful Navaho blankets. Two pairs of well-polished cowboy boots sat toe-to-toe with a braided rug, lined up so neatly that you'd almost expect a drill sergeant to march in and inspect them.

In one corner, lunge whips and braided lariats sprouted from a galvanized milk churn. In another, a pair of small leather armchairs invited her to relax. Between them, a black trunk with brass hinges held an insulated mug of apple cider and a vase of red roses.

Were those real?

She touched the petals. No, fake, but still . . .

A puff of air escaped from overstuffed cushions as Kate sat down. Behind her, draped over the back, was a knitted afghan that looked suspiciously like the ones Aunt Bea made. Kate wrapped herself up in it. Not that she needed to. This cozy little tack room was warmer than her bedroom at home.

Wide-eyed, Kate looked around.

Mr. Evans's barn had always been tidy, but this was beyond awesome. Had he spruced things up even more to make her and Tapestry feel welcome? He'd obviously made that special nameplate, and—

There was a soft knock on the door.

"Kate, are you in there?"

* * *

Holly's stomach churned, like it had last night when Aunt Bea announced her secret weapon.

Mrs. Gordon?

It made no sense. Why would The Gorgon help

Kate get back to the barn, unless it was to impress Kate's dad? Infuriatingly, Aunt Bea hadn't explained or given any more clues. She'd just told Holly to be ready by eight so they could drive to Mr. Evans's farm.

"But Kate will be there," Holly had said.

Aunt Bea nodded. "That's the whole point."

And now, here she was, knocking on Mr. Evans's tack room door and scared stiff that Kate would yank it open and then slam it shut in her face.

Slowly, it opened.

15

FOR A FEW CRAZY SECONDS, Kate's tiny corner of the world stood still—no sound of chomping from Pardner's stall or Mr. Evans's barn cat demanding attention. Even his cows had stopped mooing.

Holly?

She gave a tiny smile. "Aunt Bea made me do it."

"Yeah, I bet," Kate said, almost choking on the words. Still, it was better than bursting into tears, which she did anyway.

So did Holly.

Like the heroines from one of Holly's favorite movies, they wrapped their arms around each other and hung on as if they were the only two survivors in a sinking lifeboat.

"We ought to be cool about this," Holly said.

Kate sniffed. "Dream on."

Then Holly said, "I'm sorry," and Kate did, too, over and over, until their joined hands and their words blended together, the way they always had.

Holly wiped her eyes. "Wow, this is an epic tack room," she said, looking as wide-eyed as Kate had been a few moments earlier.

"Tell me about it," Kate said. "It's like—"

"The Dover Saddlery?"

Kate burst out laughing. Trust Holly to tap into the very same thoughts she'd had. Still holding hands, they sank into the matching leather armchairs. Holly took a swig of apple cider from the mug that Mr. Evans had left.

She sighed. "I could get used to this."

"Me, too," Kate said.

Wait a minute.

How did Holly know about the cider? Come to think of it, how had she known where to find Kate? A dozen questions surged through Kate's suspicious mind.

She pinned Holly with a look the way Aunt Bea always did. "Is this a conspiracy?"

"Um, yes."

"Okay, so who was in on it?"

"Me, Aunt Bea, Mr. Evans . . ."

"My dad?" Kate said.

Holly turned faintly pink. "Yes."

"Oh," Kate said, letting out her breath. So Dad had known all along that Holly would show up at Mr. Evans's barn while he and Mr. Evans were off getting Tapestry.

"It was Aunt Bea's idea," Holly said.

No surprise there. "Why?"

But before Holly could answer, Aunt Bea swept through the tack room door as if she'd been outside, waiting for just the right moment to intervene. She scooted Holly out of her armchair and sat down. Holly perched on its arm.

"Did you tell Kate my plan?" said Aunt Bea.

Holly shook her head. "No."

"Why not?"

"Because I don't know what it is," Holly said, swinging her leg back and forth. "All you said was that Mrs. Gordon could help us get Kate back into the barn."

"Mrs. *Gordon*?" Kate said. "Why would she help me?"

"Because she's a high school principal."

"*Was*," Holly pointed out.

"Doesn't matter," said Aunt Bea. "Parents still respect her, including Mrs. Dean."

Holly snorted. "Yeah, right. And pigs fly."

"If you're going to be disruptive, you may leave the room," Aunt Bea said, sounding just like Mrs. Gordon.

Kate giggled and nudged Holly. "Behave."

"That's rich," Holly said, "coming from you."

"Last night," said Aunt Bea, "I ran into Cecilly in the village, and—"

"Was she on a Valentine date?" Holly said.

"As a matter of fact, yes."

"Ugh." Holly pulled a face. "Who'd date *her*?"

"Mr. Gordon," Aunt Bea said. "Her husband."

"But they're getting a divorce."

"Not any more," said Aunt Bea. "They're back together again."

"Whoopee!" Holly cried. "That is *so* cool." She grabbed Kate's hand and held it up like she'd just won a prize fight.

Relief flooded through Kate like a warm wave. This day had gone from being a disaster into being the best she could possibly have. Well, almost.

"Hush," Kate said. "Let Aunt Bea talk."

"Thank you," she said. "Now, according to Cecilly, Angela was insufferably rude to Earl at The Shack. Is this true?"

"Yes," Kate said. "But I shouldn't have slapped her."

"I agree," said Aunt Bea. "Nevertheless, I doubt Mrs. Dean knows *why* you did it."

"Angela's not going to tell her," Holly said. "That's for sure."

"But Cecilly might," said Aunt Bea. "And while she's at it, she might also mention to Mrs. Dean that Angela tried to frame Kate for plagiarism last semester."

"And failed, miserably," Holly said.

"But," Kate said, "you don't really know that Mrs. Gordon would say anything, do you?"

Aunt Bea pursed her lips. "All I have to do is mention to Mrs. Dean that Mrs. Gordon knows a few things about Angela that Mrs. Dean might prefer be kept quiet, and I'm sure she'll decide that Kate belongs back at Timber Ridge."

"But that's blackmail," Holly cried.

"Exactly," said Aunt Bea. "But with someone like Mrs. Dean, it's the only thing that'll get her attention." She helped herself to the last of Kate's cider. "Remember, she's an expert at this."

Kate looked at Holly.

She grinned and gave Kate a high five

Kate grinned back. It might just work. Whenever Aunt Bea set her mind to something, it usually paid off, never mind if it was totally off the wall.

"Hello, we're back," came Mr. Evans's voice.

Kate leaped to her feet. "C'mon," she said. "Tapestry's here."

With Holly and Aunt Bea right behind, she rushed outside. Mr. Evans had lowered his trailer's ramp and was backing Tapestry out. Her mane and tail glistened, her coat shone like a newly minted penny. She looked every inch the superstar horse in her royal blue blanket and matching halter, and someone—probably Jennifer—had wrapped her legs in royal blue shipping bandages.

From the barn, Pardner whinnied.

Tapestry whinnied back. Ears pricked, she danced about and seemed eager to get inside. Maybe she could smell the fresh hay or wanted to rub noses with Pardner.

"Thank you for everything," Kate said as Mr. Evans handed her Tapestry's lead rope.

"You're welcome," he said.

Kate hugged her mare, feeling warm and fuzzy inside. "This is our new home."

Holly patted Tapestry's neck. "But not for long," she whispered. "I promise."

Don't miss **DOUBLE FEATURE, Book 9**
in the exciting **Timber Ridge Riders** series,
coming soon

Sign up for our mailing list and be among the first to
know when the next Timber Ridge Riders book
will be out.

Send your email address to:
timberridgeriders@gmail.com

For more information about the series, visit:
www.timberridgeriders.com
Note: all email addresses are kept strictly confidential

About the Author

MAGGIE DANA'S FIRST RIDING LESSON, at the age of five, was less than wonderful. She hated it so much, she didn't try again for another three years. But all it took was the right horse and the right instructor and she was hooked.

After that, Maggie begged for her own pony and was lucky enough to get one. Smoky was a black New Forest pony who loved to eat vanilla pudding and drink tea, and he became her constant companion. Maggie even rode him to school one day and tethered him to the bicycle rack . . . but not for long because all the other kids wanted pony rides, much to their teachers' dismay.

Maggie and Smoky competed in Pony Club trials and won several ribbons. But mostly, they had fun—trail riding and hanging out with other horse-crazy girls. At horse camp, Maggie and her teammates spent one night sleeping in the barn, except they didn't get much sleep because the horses snored. The next morning, everyone was tired and cranky, especially when told to jump without stirrups.

Born and raised in England, Maggie now makes her home on the Connecticut shoreline. When not mucking stalls or grooming shaggy ponies, Maggie enjoys spending time with her family and writing the next book in her TIMBER RIDGE RIDERS series.